BRIDGE ACROSS ASIA

FAVORITE ASIAN STORIES

PENNY CAMERON

Language & Culture Center
University of Houston

Dominie Press, Inc.

Publisher: Raymond Yuen
Content Editor: Holly Eubanks
Copy Editor: Becky Colgan
Illustrator: Paul Lee
Text Layout: Becky Colgan

Published by

Dominie Press, Inc.
1949 Kellogg Avenue
Carlsbad, CA 92008

www.dominie.com

ISBN 1-56270-046-4
Printed in U.S.A.

4 5 6 7 8 00

CONTENTS

ACKNOWLEDGMENTS

The author would like to thank the following people for their help and advice:

Carol Archer	Houston, Texas
Widiana Hartawan	Houston, Texas
Takaaki Inoue	Houston, Texas
Babar Jamal	Houston, Texas
Hong Yuan Lui	Houston, Texas
Jamal Mapar	Houston, Texas
Kwanruan Pinitpan	Houston, Texas

INTRODUCTION TO THE TEACHER

The Stories

hese stories were chosen for their familiarity to students from different parts of Asia. It is often hard to pin them to any one location because they deal with universal themes. "The Story of the Mount of Anticipation, Mother-Son Mountain" from Vietnam explains the shape of a particular rock formation. There is a similar story about a rock formation known as Amah Rock in Hong Kong, and indeed there are thousands of other stories that explain why things look the way they do in a manner appropriate to the culture and history of the storytellers. The moon has generated many stories that explain why it looks and behaves as it does. In this selection we have "The Woodcutter in the Moon from China" and "Why the Moon Goes Away" from Thailand.

Stories travel, too. "The Flying Fairy Wife" from Korea is similar to a story from the Philippines. Both probably stem from an old Chinese story. The theme of goodness rewarded and evil punished appears in "The Story of White Onion and Red Onion," which is an Indonesian Cinderella story, and in "The Woodcutter in the Moon." "The Elves Help an Old Man," from Japan, which also has a Korean version, teaches the listener or reader not to be envious of the good fortune of others. It can also be used to teach the students not to be too preoccupied with physical appearance, which is the thrust of some of the questions after the story. "How Vietnamese People Discovered Watermelons" teaches us that people can be foolish, be punished, and then rediscover their own talents.

"The Golden Swan" from Laos shows that good fortune must not be exploited irresponsibly, and "The Story of Brave Kong" from Cambodia ironically shows how fortune can be fickle and fall upon the wrong person. The saga of Rama and Sita is a story of the triumph of good over evil.

"The Legend of Magdapio" from the Philippines is a Romeo and Juliet story that explains a feature of the landscape. Finally, "The Animals of the Chinese Zodiac" were included because most Asian students already know the animal sign of their year of birth.

These stories were told long ago, and they reflect the attitudes of their time. Thus a villager can say to Brave Kong, "Women can't kill tigers," although

Kong's two wives have just done so. (Let him try such a falsehood today!) Kong is seen to consult with his wives throughout the story, and we all know where the real power lies. A modern Brave Kong is Flashman, an English anti-hero invented by George MacDonald Fraser, who likewise wins for all the wrong reasons. Brave Kong, ironic even in its title, is the story of an idler who never does anything to justify his success. Cambodian students laugh at him, and so should we all, for we all know that his lifestyle is not going to bring rewards in the real world.

The criteria for choosing these stories included the number of students who instantly recognized them or knew a similar story and a concern to balance the themes of the stories. (It would be possible to fill a book with stories of any of the types represented above.) Students will be pleased when they recognize a story. Their enthusiasm in recounting another version and the discussion that the stories engender makes this a rewarding experience. It is impossible to get a traditional story right (only the student's grandmother can do that), and we owe a tremendous debt to the people who have passed these stories down, generation after generation. What a shame it would be if we let them die now.

Teachers who have used *Bridge Across the Americas* will recognize the thrust of the comments that follow. The reasoning behind *Bridge Across Asia* is the same. If we give students stories from their own cultures, they will recognize them. They will have more motivation to induce meaning, they will anticipate more, and they will feel they have something to contribute to the discussion. Most students who come from other cultures are caught up in the stories, and they remember stories with similar themes from their own literary heritage. After all, nearly everyone has a story to explain the presence of the man or hare or boy or children in the moon.

Rationale

 ecent reading research suggests that students will learn to read more easily if we activate their schemata before they start to work on a text. (A schema is the knowledge of the world a person has accumulated in a lifetime. Schemata is the plural form.) Such activation of their schemata will let the students bring what they know to the text and interact with it.

The illustrations should give the reader a preview of the story, and there should be prereading questions and activities to appropriately direct the reader's attention. Students can then employ top-down reading strategies, working from whole to part, and making intelligent guesses at individual lexical items. For example, students who know the story of "The Flying Fairy Wife" know her sadness at being separated from her family. They are likely to be able to deduce the meaning of *homesick* even if they have not encountered the word before. They can also employ bottom-up strategies; for example, they will reason that to be homesick is to miss your home so much it is like sickness. They are working from part to whole, another valid way to seek meaning.

The rationale behind these stories and exercises, written primarily but not exclusively for people who have ties to Asia, follows:

- People learn to read by using what they know. These stories have been chosen for their familiarity, so the students will feel at home.

- Students must be actively involved in the reading task. At the beginning of a story, students will be challenged to deduce the meaning of some vocabulary items by completing a task, like a matching exercise, or suggesting words that relate to a particular topic. This preteaching is intended to make the students participate in learning the meanings of new words, not just copy definitions. It is best done as a cooperative learning exercise and should be checked before the story is read. Word lists and semantic maps may usefully be presented on the chalkboard.

- Traditional stories are suitable for both children and adults. We can have a high degree of confidence that traditional stories will be familiar to the largest possible segment of Asian students.

- Traditional stories have simple story grammars. The narrative structure has been refined over the years, and the expository structures are clear. For example, a traditional story will not indulge in flashbacks (the narrative proceeds in chronological order).

- The exercises are designed to let students employ top-down and bottom-up strategies. They are varied, so the student will have to think, not simply learn how to do the same exercise over and over. The questions and exercises will include discussion of the illustrations to activate the students' schemata. There are oral and written questions to involve the students in the story and comprehension and vocabulary questions but they will not always take the same form.

- Some of the students who read these stories will come from cultures where a particular traditional story does not exist or exists in a different form. The questions about the illustrations are designed to prevent the student from engaging the wrong schema.

- Internal glosses of key words help the reader. Wherever possible, a new word will be explained within the text (for example, "He knows he's blushing, because his face is red and hot.")

- Students are encouraged to reread the text when answering questions. They should use the context and not regard the exercises as memory tests.

- The stories are short, to give a sense of fulfillment—a quick reward.

- The syntax is controlled. Sentences are short, and figurative language is avoided. Passives and subjunctives are avoided (wherever possible, although *wish*, *want*, and *think* are used.

- The stories are graduated in difficulty; those at the beginning of the book are easier than those at the end.

It is impossible to separate vocabulary from comprehension at high beginner/low intermediate levels. The prereading activities introduce new vocabulary, the postreading questions enlarge upon it, and the discussion and invention questions provide an opportunity for using the new words. Comprehension questions and exercises usually involve group work. These questions range from those that can be answered directly from the text to those that draw upon the students' own experiences. Because the students will have limited language to express themselves, discussion and invention questions are simple and relevant to the story and/or the students' lives.

Dictation is far more than a mere spelling test. It is a quick test of global competence. However, if the students are reading the dictation before you give it to them, all is not lost. Tell the students to read the passage to you. Then transcribe what they say onto the chalkboard *exactly as you hear it,* pausing to accept self-correction by the student or correction by other members of the class.

Strategies in the Classroom

 ou can do what a book cannot—perceive the strengths and needs of the student. The prereading questions are intended to activate the readers' schemata, to make them apply what they know to the text. The exercises in the Using What You Know section are designed to provide some of the vocabulary your students will need.

No teacher should feel limited by what is in a text. If you think of questions or activities that will trigger something in the minds of your students, use them. You know your class better than anyone else.

If at all possible, read the story aloud to your class and have them read along with you silently. Students learn a great deal about suprasegmental features such as pitch, pace, emphasis, and rhythm by listening to the teacher read. Reading aloud helps the students to understand the story and to avoid miscues.

It is helpful if students read the story at least twice before they try to answer the questions. Read the story aloud while the students follow and mark unfamiliar words. Immediately read the story again and ask the students to flag words that are still unfamiliar after the second reading. The number of unknown words is usually reduced by 50 percent simply by reading twice, and this is not lost on the students. Alternatively, the students may read the story silently in class before you read to them, or they may read it as a homework assignment and read it aloud themselves in class. Students may be asked to identify their favorite part of the story and to read it aloud.

Some students resist the idea of reading to the end of a sentence to get clues to unknown words. The following exercise may help. Write on the board:

Let's go _____ (fishing, shopping, flying, swimming).
Let's go _____ (fishing, shopping, flying, swimming) in the mall.

Ask the students which word is right in the second sentence. Ask them how they know. You may want to repeat the exercise with other sentences, for example:

I like to _____ (eat, drive, run, finish).
I like to _____ (eat, drive, run, finish) my car.
I want a _____ (tiger, tree, fan, mountain).
I want a _____ (tiger, tree, fan, mountain) to put in my garden.

ESL students are often very slow to respond to a question. Wilson and Cleland suggest waiting three to five seconds, thus allowing students time to think and form their responses and to elaborate on them.

When an exercise calls for a pictorial response, encourage the students to draw quickly. Stick figures are ideal. The value of the exercise lies in the explanation of the drawing to other students. Pictorial responses may be done as small group or blackboard exercise.

The last point is really made by the stories themselves. They happen to be a lot of fun, and for this we must thank the storytellers who passed them down to us, honing and refining them at every telling, century after century.

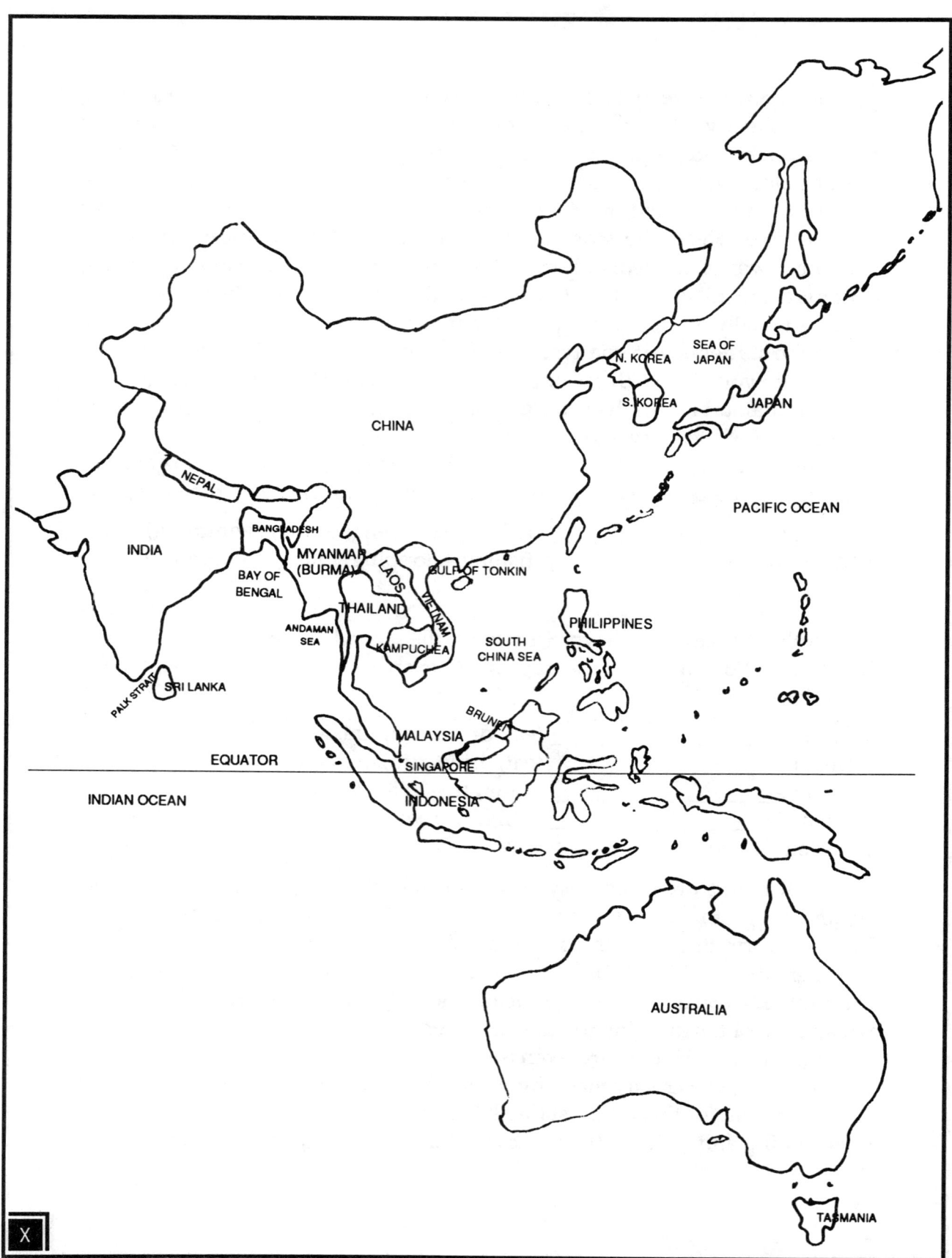

CHINA

N. KOREA

SEA OF JAPAN

S. KOREA

JAPAN

PACIFIC OCEAN

NEPAL

BANGLADESH

INDIA

MYANMAR (BURMA)

BAY OF BENGAL

LAOS

GULF OF TONKIN

THAILAND

VIETNAM

PHILIPPINES

ANDAMAN SEA

KAMPUCHEA

SOUTH CHINA SEA

PALK STRAIT

SRI LANKA

BRUNEI

MALAYSIA

EQUATOR

SINGAPORE

INDIAN OCEAN

INDONESIA

AUSTRALIA

TASMANIA

X

READING THE MAP

The **border** between two countries is the line where one country stops and the next country begins. You can see the border between Thailand and Cambodia on the map.

Climate describes the weather you expect in a particular place. Thailand has a hot climate. Japan is further from the equator, so it has a cooler climate.

A **coast** is the land next to the sea. Another word that means the same is **seashore**.

A **compass** is used to show direction. The directions on the compass are north, south, east and west. The sun rises in the east and sets in the west. Look at the map. Japan is north of the Philippines and east of China.

The **equator** is an imaginary line running around the middle of the earth. It is very hot on the equator.

An **island** is a piece of land completely surrounded by water. An island can be big, like Sri Lanka, or small, like the many little islands that make up the Philippines.

A **mainland** is a large land mass without its islands.

An **ocean** is a very large body of salt water. The biggest ocean is the Pacific Ocean.

A **peninsula** is a piece of land surrounded on three sides by water. Look at Korea. It is a peninsula.

A **sea** is a large body of salt water and is usually part of an ocean. The Sea of Japan is part of the Pacific Ocean.

A **strait** is a narrow passage of water between two pieces of land.

How Vietnamese People Discovered Watermelons

Before You Read

- Answer the following questions.

  1. What is a watermelon?
  2. What do you see in the illustration? What do you think is happening? (There are no absolutely right answers to this question.)

- Find Vietnam on the map at the front of the book. Then correct the mistakes in this passage about Vietnam.

Vietnam is a town in Asia. Its nearest neighbors are China, which is on its southern border, and Laos and Cambodia, which are west of Vietnam. The

Gulf of Tongking, which is part of the Atlantic Ocean, is to the east of Vietnam. The country is close to the equator, so it is very hot. The language of Vietnam is called Spanish, although some Vietnamese people speak Cantonese, which is the language of southern China.

Helpful Information

Vietnam has a very long history. Here is a diagram:

2879 B.C.	111 B.C.	A.D. 939	A.D. 1884	A.D. 1955
Legendary time	Chinese domination	Independent period	French domination	Modern period

What does B.C. mean? What does A.D. mean? See if anyone in your class knows. You can find out from your dictionary or from the library.

- How many years passed between 2879 B.C. and A.D. 1955?
- Our story is set in 258 B.C. How long ago is that?

Using What You Know

1. The *mainland* means
   a. a group of islands
   b. a large land mass without its islands

2. Think of all the words and phrases that you know that relate to being on a deserted island. Write them below. Two examples are given.

   do things for myself
   alone

3. How could you live on a deserted island? What sort of things would you need?

ong, long ago there was an emperor of Vietnam called Hung Vuong VIII. He died in the year 258 B.C., and our story happened in the last years of his life.

The emperor had an adopted son called An Tiem. He loved the young man dearly and helped him in everything he did. When it was time for An Tiem to marry, the emperor found a good wife for him. The young couple lived happily, and the emperor gave them everything they wanted or needed. They had servants to look after them. Their house was beautiful, and their food was delicious. However, everyone knew it was a gift from the emperor.

One day An Tiem and his wife were walking in the garden.

"This is so beautiful," the wife said. "You are clever, my dear."

A gardener was working nearby. He expected An Tiem to say, "It's all a gift from the emperor," but he didn't. Instead he said, "Yes, I am clever, aren't I?" The young couple laughed and went away.

Another time someone heard An Tiem say, "Look at my house! All this is the result of hard work."

Of course, it wasn't long before people told the emperor. The old man was furious.

"Bring An Tiem here immediately!" he shouted.

An Tiem came to the palace. The emperor asked, "Do you like your house?"

"Of course," An Tiem replied. "It's a lovely place." He was very puzzled. Why did the emperor ask?

"I believe you earned it by your hard work," the emperor went on. His voice was icy.

"Of course not, Father," An Tiem replied. And then he realized that someone had told about his silly joke. He opened his mouth to speak, but the emperor spoke first.

"I will show you what hard work is," he said. "You are no longer my son. You are ungrateful! You and your wife and child will live on a deserted island. Go!"

So An Tiem and his little family went to the island. There was nothing on it—no hut, no house, and worst of all, no people. They had to learn how to look after themselves.

The little family found life very difficult at first. They had to build a house and find food in the jungle. But after a while they learned how to live quite comfortably.

One summer day some birds flew in from the east. They left behind some seeds, which soon grew. The plant was a vine that ran over a lot of ground. The fruit was very large, with a dark green skin. Inside it was a beautiful pink. The fruit was very sweet to eat.

An Tiem cared for the watermelon vines, and the family enjoyed the fruit. One day a small junk came to the island, and An Tiem let the sailors taste the fruit.

"This is delicious," the captain of the junk said.

An Tiem said, "I will trade some of this fruit with you. What do you have on your boat?"

The captain and An Tiem bargained. An Tiem held up a watermelon, and the captain said, "I have some very fine rice." Then they argued about how much rice a watermelon was worth.

At the end of the day the junk sailed away full of watermelons. An Tiem and his family had new clothes and fine rice. They were very pleased to have things they could not make themselves, like needles and cooking pots.

Soon the word spread, and An Tiem and his family did good business. Junks came from the mainland with goods to exchange for watermelons. The little family had iron cooking pots, beautiful vases, and fine china. After a while they became quite rich.

The emperor missed An Tiem badly. One day he said to his messengers, "Go and find out what happened to An Tiem. I'm worried about him. I'm sure he could not look after himself on that island. Maybe he's dead."

A messenger left the palace to look for An Tiem. He went down to the sea, and the sailors said, "An Tiem? Yes, we know him. He's the rich man who lives on the island with delicious fruit." So the messenger went to the island. He was very surprised to see how well An Tiem and his family were living.

The messenger went back to the emperor. "An Tiem and his wife and family are well," he said. "He has built a good house, and they are very comfortable."

"So, he has done well without me," the emperor thought. "I miss seeing his face." He said aloud, "Go to the island. Bring An Tiem and his family to me."

An Tiem and his wife and child came to the palace and bowed low.

"You may rise," the emperor said. "What is in that basket?"

"I have brought you a piece of fruit," An Tiem said.

"It's very large," the emperor replied. He ordered the palace cook to cut the watermelon up. The cook brought back large slices of the pink melon, and the emperor ate it until the juice ran down his chin.

"This is delicious," the emperor said. "You can come back now, An Tiem. Bring your family. You are my son again."

"Thank you, Father," An Tiem replied politely.

So the family came back and lived near the emperor's palace. The emperor sent melon seeds to all the people, and soon everyone in Vietnam was enjoying watermelon.

The emperor named the island An Tiem, in honor of his clever adopted son. ▲

Understanding What You Read

1. Circle the words that best complete the sentences.

   An Tiem was the emperor's (1. eldest, only, adopted) son. The emperor helped An Tiem and his wife with (2. very little, nothing, everything). Then the emperor heard that An Tiem said he earned his home by hard work. The emperor was (3. delighted, furious, unhappy), and he sent An Tiem and his family to a deserted (4. beach, mountain, island). An Tiem discovered (5. oranges, grapes, watermelons) and traded with people on the (6. mainland, mountain, street). He grew rich. At last the emperor called An Tiem back to live on the (7. mainland, island, river) again.

2. Why do you think the emperor was so angry? Pretend you are the emperor. Write the decree to banish An Tiem and give the reasons why you are sending him away. Work with a partner or a group.

Vocabulary

Find the meaning for each word. Then write the letters of the correct meanings on the lines.

_____e_____	1. mainland	a.	argue over a price
_____	2. gift	b.	gain by working
_____	3. clever	c.	Asian boat
_____	4. earn	d.	house for a king or emperor
_____	5. junk	e.	large mass of land
_____	6. bargain	f.	smart, intelligent
_____	7. palace	g.	present

Discussion and Writing

How Events in the Story Reveal Character

What sort of person was An Tiem? We could say he was foolish, because he made a silly joke that lost him his beautiful first home. Talk with your classmates and find other events in the story that show what sort of man he was. Make a list below.

_____

_____

_____

_____

Tell It Your Way

1. Do you know any stories like this one? If so, tell the story to your partner or class.
2. Role-play An Tiem bargaining with the captain of the junk. You may make notes on what you will say.

Outside the Story

An Tiem and his family were pleased to have things they could not make themselves. Look around the room and describe one thing in it that you *can* make yourself. Say what it is used for, what it looks like, and how you can make it.

OR

Describe your favorite personal possession. Explain why you value it so highly.

Library Work: Time

How do people from different countries count time? English-speaking countries use Before Christ (B.C.) for the time before Christ was born and Anno Domino (A.D.) for the years after Christ's birth. But how do people in Muslim countries, or in China, count time? Ask your classmates, or go to the library and look for the information. Make notes on any other ways you find of counting the years.

Listening: Which Word Did You Hear Twice?

Many words in English have just one sound that makes them different from another word. Your hip is the joint at the top of your leg; a heap is a pile of something, like a heap of dirty clothes ready for the laundry. You must be careful to make them sound different.

Below you will find a list of words with just one sound difference. Your teacher will read the words to you, repeating one of the words twice. Circle the word that you hear twice. For example, if your teacher reads, "slip, sleep, slip," you will circle the word *slip*.

slip	sleep
chip	cheap
pip	peep
rip	reap

sip	seep
whip	weep
dip	deep
ship	sheep

Game: What's That Word?

One person, the challenger, secretly chooses a word and writes a dash on a piece of paper for each letter in the word. The other players try to guess what the letters in the word are. If a player suggests a letter that is not in the word, the challenger gets a point. If a player suggests a correct letter, the challenger must write that letter in the right place in the word. Players have ten chances to find the letters in the word. If they think they know the word, they can suggest the whole word.

Why the Moon Goes Away

Before You Read

- Answer the following questions.

    1. What does the title make you expect in this story?
    2. What do you see in the illustration? Can you guess what has happened? (There are no absolutely right answers to this question.)
    3. Draw a chariot on the chalkboard. What is it used for?

- Find Thailand on the map at the front of the book. Then correct the mistakes in this passage about Thailand.

Thailand is surrounded by France to the north and west, by Laos to the northeast, and by Cambodia to the south and east. The northern part of Thailand is a peninsula that goes down to the border with Singapore. The country is close to the equator, so it is very cool. The Andaman Sea lies east of Thailand.

Helpful Information

The Thai people came to Thailand from southern China. At first they came slowly, but in the thirteenth century the Mongols ruled China. Many Thai people fled from the Yunnan region through the hills into Thailand.

• Can you tell the class anything else about Thailand?

Using What You Know

Think of all the words that you know that relate to the moon and write them in the column on the left. Write words that relate to the sun in the column on the right.

moon	sun

here was once a beautiful young woman called Tatsani. She was a princess in Thailand before the storytellers first began to tell their tales, at a time when Thailand was called Siam. It was so long ago that the sky was very low, and people had to push it up when they went outside. It was so long ago that there was no moon, and the stars were very bright and very lonely. This story tells how the stars found their moon.

Princess Tatsani was born in the palace of her parents, the king and queen of Siam. Her father ruled the whole earth, while the Sun King ruled the heavens. Tatsani's mother, the queen of Siam, loved her daughter dearly. She taught Tatsani how to dance and how to be a true princess, gentle and kind. Tatsani learned her lessons so well that even the stars in heaven loved her.

While Tatsani was a child the whole world was happy and at peace, and people had time to enjoy all the good things in the world. The royal family watched the little girl as she played. "The little princess is growing more beautiful every day," a woman told the queen. The queen watched Tatsani playing in the palace garden and saw that it was true. "The child has a sweet nature," the queen thought. "I wonder what her life will be like? Will she be a caring, gracious person? Or will she be spoiled and selfish?"

When Tatsani became a woman, she was so beautiful that everyone who saw her fell in love with her. People spoke of her kindness, and nobody could say an evil word about her. But this same goodness and beauty brought terrible sadness to every living creature on the earth.

Every morning the Sun King, who ruled the heavens, drove his golden chariot across the sky and brought light to the people on the earth below. Every evening he returned to his home behind the clouds so that night could fall and the people could rest in the dark. But one fateful day, the Sun King drove past the palace and saw Tatsani. Like everyone else, he fell in love with her.

The Sun King stopped his chariot in its flight across the sky. "I must look into that wonderful face again," he thought. He drove around the palace to look for Tatsani. When he found her, he stayed above the palace garden so that he could watch her and see how gently she touched the flowers and how gracefully she moved.

The sun beat down and made the garden too hot, so Tatsani went inside. The Sun King kept driving around the palace, waiting for her to come out again. He was so in love that he did not realize that it was much too hot for any living thing to stay near his fiery chariot. The earth became dry and scorched, and the river beds dried up. The mud cracked. As the plants died in the cruel heat, the water in the rice fields evaporated, and the rice began to dry out. The people waited and prayed for the Sun King to go away, but still he stayed outside the palace.

At last, very frightened, the people of Siam came to see their king. "We will all die," they cried. "The crops are failing, so there will be nothing for us to eat. But worse still, our water supply is drying up. We are tired, sire, for we cannot sleep. The sun is always blazing in the sky, so it's midday all the time. We long for the cool and darkness of the night, but it never comes. We are afraid that the Sun King will not go away until he has seen Tatsani. What is to become of us?"

The poor stars in the sky cried to the king, "We can never come out, because the day never ends. How can we play in a bright blue sky? We need the night, with its beautiful black sky."

The King of Siam held his head and tried to think of a way he could approach the Sun King. How could he save his daughter? If she went away, the Sun King would leave the palace, and the world would be put to rights. But he loved Tatsani too dearly to send her away.

Tatsani, the innocent cause of all this trouble, was as miserable as everyone else. "I can go to the cave behind my father's palace," she thought. "It will be cool and quiet deep inside the mountain, and maybe I can think what to do." She left the palace and hurried to the cave. The Sun King saw his chance and flew down to follow her inside. He left his chariot outside the cave and ran after her on foot.

The Sun King fell on his knees before Tatsani and told her how much he loved her—how he wanted her to be his queen. The light from outside the cave grew dimmer, and then it became dark. Tatsani and the Sun King hurried to the front of the cave. It was nighttime! The stars were out playing in the black sky, and the Sun King's golden chariot was nowhere to be seen.

"Where's my chariot?" the Sun King cried out in alarm.

The stars gave little silvery laughs, but they kept on playing.

"I can't stay here on earth. I don't belong here!" the Sun King said. He was so unhappy it was very difficult for him to speak. The stars took no notice, and the poor Sun King became more and more frantic. At last he broke down and cried.

Tatsani could not bear to see him so distressed, and she wept with him. Tatsani's tears turned to silver while the King's turned to gold, and these two precious metals were locked inside the earth.

The stars moved uneasily in the sky, for they hated to see their beloved Tatsani cry. At last one star called out, "Sun King! Will you listen to us? We know where your chariot is."

The Sun King said, "Of course I will listen. You can understand my problem, little stars. I cannot stay on earth, and without the chariot I cannot go home. Who will control the sunlight? Who will make the days begin and end?"

"You must make two promises," the stars said. "Then we will let you have your chariot."

"What are they?" the Sun King asked, and Tatsani held her breath.

"First, you must go home at the end of every day," the stars said.

"I agree to that," the Sun King said. "I shall build a home behind the clouds for Tatsani, and I'll go home to her."

"Secondly, we love Tatsani too," the stars said. "We want to have her for half of every month. We want her to be our moon."

Tatsani could see that this was fair, and she smiled at the Sun King. He said, "I agree. And when the moon is not in the sky, and the sun is down, she and I can be in our home together."

And so sweet Tatsani goes for two weeks to be with the stars in the night. The rest of the month she lives with her husband, the fiery Sun King so that the people of the earth may sleep. ▲

Understanding What You Read

- Answer the following questions.
    1. When did this story happen?
    2. Why did the day never end?
    3. What did the stars suggest to solve the problem?

- How can you tell that this story takes place a long time ago? Find parts of the story that show it is very old.

Vocabulary

Find words in the story that describe Tatsani. Use them to make her name. We've started for you:

B E A U **T** I F U L

        A

        T

        S

        A

        N

        I

Compare your list with what other people have written.

Discussion and Writing

"While Tatsani was a child . . . people had time to enjoy all the good things in the world."

1. What good things do you have time to enjoy? What do you miss because you don't have time to enjoy them? Talk with other people, and make a list. Compare your ideas with other people in the class.

Things we enjoy in our spare time	Things we miss because we don't have time to enjoy them

2. Do you know any other stories about the moon or the stars? Tell the class.

3. People love to tell stories about the moon because it's a way to explain why the moon looks the way it does. Look at the ink blots on page 15 carefully (you may turn the page any way you like) and write sentences about them. Here are some beginnings to sentences you might like to use:

It looks like . . .
It reminds me of . . .
It's just like . . .
Perhaps it's a . . .
I think I see a . . .

Look at the sentences written by other class members. How are they different from yours? Are any of them the same?

Tell It Your Way

1. Divide the class into two groups. One group tells the story the way the Sun King sees it. The other group tells the story from the viewpoint of the people in the village. Tell each story to the class. Why are the two stories different from each other?
2. What would happen if Tatsani and the Sun King refused the stars' suggestion? Make another ending to this story.
3. Would you say that this is a love story? Give your evidence from the story.

Outside the Story

Library Work: Research

1. Find out more about Thailand. How is the country governed? What are the principal exports? What are the buildings like?
2. Find the story of Phaeton, the son of the Greek Sun God Apollo. What happened when Phaeton drove his father's chariot?

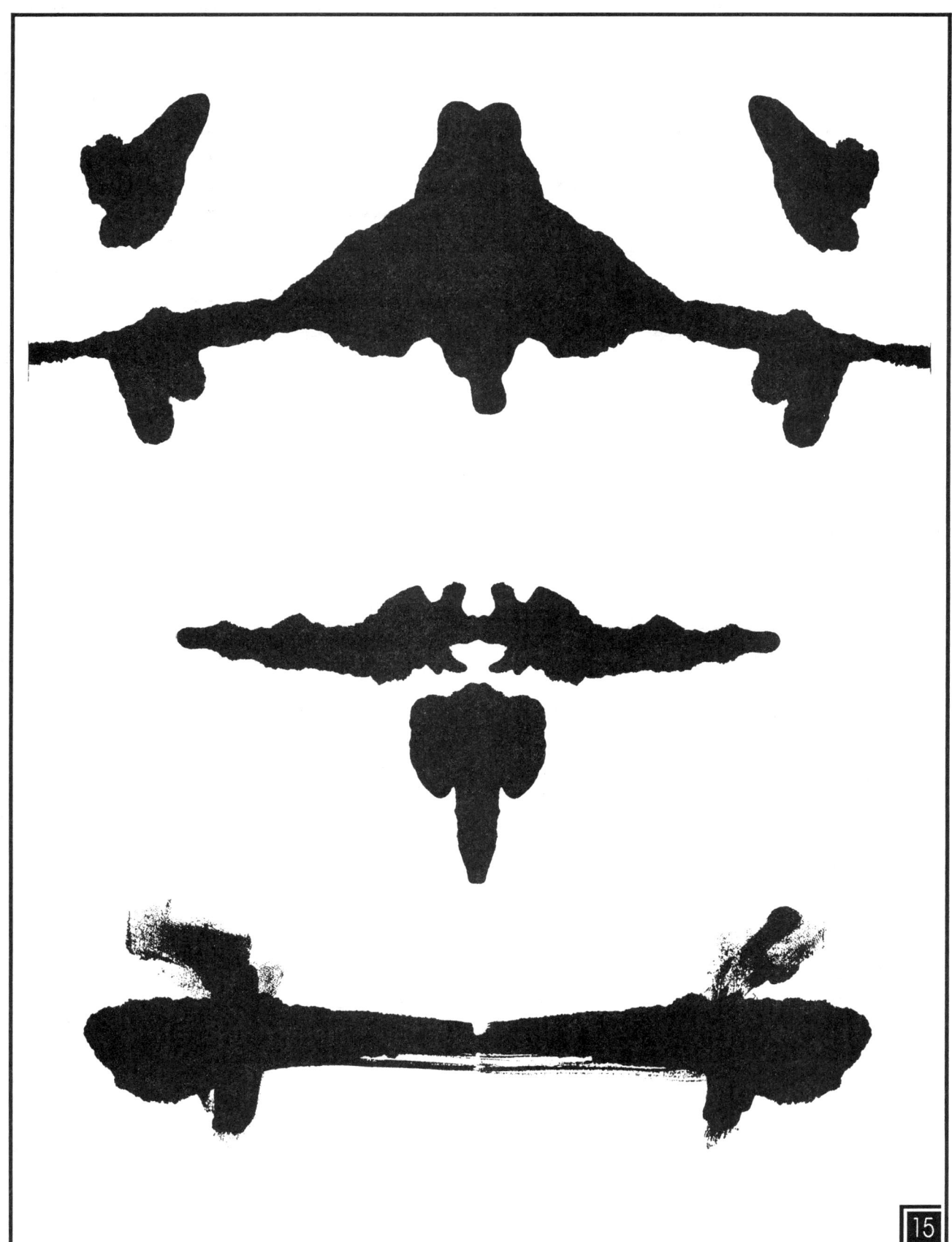

15

Listening: Which Word Did You Hear Twice?

Many words in English have just one sound that makes them different from another word. Below you will find a list of words with just one sound difference. Your teacher will read the words to you, repeating one of the words twice. Circle the word that you hear twice. For example, if your teacher reads, "feed, fed, fed," you will circle the word *fed*.

fed	feed	bled	bleed
fell	feel	men	mean
met	meat	set	seat
said	seed	check	cheek
says	sees	bet	beat

Dictation

_____

_____

_____

_____

_____

_____

_____

THE STORY OF THE MOUNT OF ANTICIPATION, MOTHER-SON MOUNTAIN

Before You Read

- Answer the following questions.

  1. What does the title make you expect in this story?
  2. What do you see in the illustration? How does the woman feel? Where is she, and what is she doing there? Can you guess what has happened? (There are no absolutely right answers to this question.)
  3. What do you know about Vietnam? Have you read the story *How Vietnamese People Discovered Watermelons?*

- Look at Vietnam on the map. Think about the legendary time in Vietnam, more than 2,000 years ago. What countries do you think Vietnam traded with? How did the Vietnamese merchants move their goods from one place to another?

Using What You Know

Some of these words are about the way people feel, and the others relate to the sea. Divide them into two columns.

grief   restless   boat   glad   joy
sail   sailor   cheerful   ship

words about feelings	words about the sea

here is a mountain in Vietnam that people call both the Mount of Anticipation and Mother-Son Mountain. Over many, many thousands of years the sea and wind have carved the rocks at the top of the mountain, changing their shape a little each day. Now the rocks look like a mother and her baby looking out across the Pacific Ocean. They are there forever, watching and waiting for someone to come home from the sea.

The Vietnamese people say the mountain is there to remind us about a good wife. Everyone said that once she was very fortunate. Her husband loved her dearly and was glad to be at her side. When their son was born, it seemed no greater joy could come. The mother cared for her husband and son and sang softly as she did her work. The baby lay in his cradle or rode cheerfully on his mother's back, the center of a loving world.

The husband, however, was a restless man, who found it very hard to settle down in one place. Sometimes he climbed the mountain to look at the sea and remembered the time before he was married. "The sea was kind to me before," he thought. "Maybe I will sail again another day." But every time he climbed that mountain he came home with greater joy to play with his child and to be with the woman he loved. He knew he was luckier and happier than he had ever been before. Then, on an ordinary day, just like any other, he made a dreadful discovery.

The husband wept alone. He kept his terrible news to himself, for he knew the painful thing he was destined to do. He must leave his family and never return. But how could he go? He would surely break his wife's heart, and her tears would burn him like boiling oil. And what if she asked why he must leave? He could not tell his secret. No, he had to creep away silently in the night, that very evening, while he had the courage.

After their evening meal, the man came to look at his baby son. The boy was asleep in his cradle, and a little smile passed across his face. The father prayed that his boy would have a happy life and that he would always find joy in things that were close to him. Then he went back to his wife.

She was sitting in the moonlight, letting her day end quietly. When she heard his footsteps, she smiled at him and said, "Isn't it a lovely night?"

Her husband looked at her and wanted to run and take her in his arms. He controlled himself sternly and said, "I would like to be alone for a little while."

His wife got up slowly. "I'm very tired," she said. "I think I'll go to bed." The man watched her walk away, her long hair swaying as she moved.

The man listened until he was sure his wife was asleep. He stood near her bed and looked at her. Then he turned away and left his home, crying silently as he walked toward the sea.

The next day the woman awoke, but her man was not beside her. She searched everywhere for him, but it did no good. Carrying her baby son, she ran to the village and asked everyone she saw, but nobody had seen her husband.

For weeks she searched, but to no avail. The woman grew thin and strange in her grief, refusing food and wandering about the village in the night. The people there were very worried about her. "It's very difficult," they said, "For a woman who loved her man so much not to know where he is." Then a sailor came to the town and said that he had seen the missing man.

The wife was happy and full of questions. "Is he well?" she cried. "Is he safe? Has he eaten enough? Oh, please, where is he? I must go to him at once."

The sailor looked at the ground and moved around uncomfortably. Then he said, "I don't know where he is now. He sailed to the east, about a month ago."

The poor woman was mad, entirely crazed with grief. She took her little son and climbed the mountain so that they could look out toward the ocean. She prayed for her husband to return. Day in and day out she waited. She neither ate nor drank; but all day, day after day after day, she stood and watched the sea. She prayed to the gods for a glimpse of her husband's ship, just one tiny look so she could see that he was coming home. If she could just see the sails and know he was still alive . . . Perhaps he was sailing home, even now.

At last the gods took pity on her. They turned both mother and son into shiny rocks looking over the water of the Pacific Ocean, waiting forever. ▲

Understanding What You Read

Read the following three accounts of the story, and choose the one that is the most accurate. Be prepared to explain your choice to the rest of the class.

1. There once was a happy family of a father, mother, and baby boy. However, the father was a thief; and one day he ran away. The people in the village knew why he had gone, but they could not stop him. His wife found out where he was and went to the mountain top to meet him.

2. There once was a happy family of a father, mother, and baby boy. One day something terrible happened, and the father ran away. His wife missed him sadly and went to a mountain top to watch for him. The gods finally pitied her and turned her into stone.

3. There once was a happy family of a father, mother, and baby boy. One day the baby got sick, and the father went away to sea to get him some medicine. The mother took her baby to the mountain top so that she could see her husband coming home.

Vocabulary

Crossword puzzle

Make up the clues to go with this crossword puzzle:

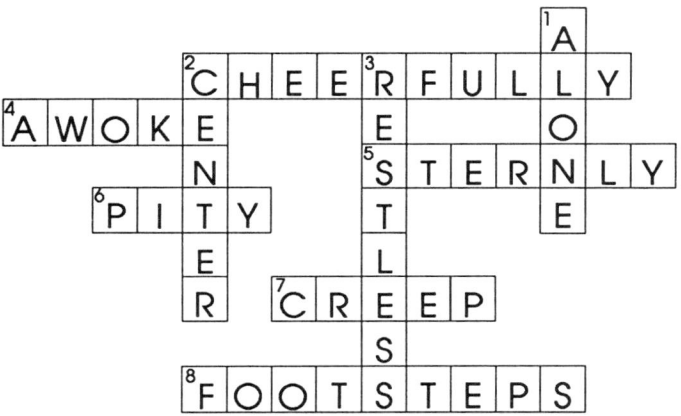

Across	Down
2. *in a very happy way*	1.
4.	2.
5.	3.
6.	
7.	
8.	

Tic-Tac-Toe

You should be in two teams. Team A has 30 seconds to choose a square and make up a sentence using the word in that square. Team B has 30 seconds to decide whether the sentence is correct and, if not, to correct it. The teacher will put an A next to the word in the grid if the sentence was really correct. If it was wrong, and Team B corrected it properly, the teacher will put a B next to the word. The first team to get three letters in a row, diagonally, vertically, or horizontally, wins.

softly	silently	dreadful
shiny	sternly	fortunate
safe	ordinary	glad

Discussion and Writing

Why do you think the man felt he had to leave his family? Talk with your classmates and write a story that tries to explain why he left home.

Survey

Ask your classmates how they feel about the man's actions. Fill out two charts: one for the men and boys and one for the women and girls.

Men and boys	Strongly agree			Strongly disagree
	1	2	3	4
• It is never right to desert people. • The woman was wrong to take her baby to the mountain top. • The man did not really love his family.				

Women and girls	Strongly agree			Strongly disagree
	1	2	3	4
• It is never right to desert people. • The woman was wrong to take her baby to the mountain top. • The man did not really love his family.				

What are the differences between what the women and girls thought and what the men and boys thought? Why do you and your classmates think these differences exist? Write your answers below.

The differences were

This may be because

Role-Play

Pretend you are the woman in the story, and you are talking to the other people in the village about your husband. Do the role-play in two scenes: first, when the woman is happy; and second, a month after the husband has run away. The other people in the group can pretend to be the villagers.

Tell It Your Way

Just as the man was creeping away from home, the baby cried and his wife woke up. "Where are you going?" she asked her husband. "Why are you crying?"

Make up a story showing what happened next. What did they say to each other? Did he go away? How can they solve the problem?

Outside the Story

Listening: Which Word Did You Hear Twice?

Many words in English have just one sound that makes them different from another word. Below you will find a list of words with just one sound difference. Your teacher will read the words to you, repeating one of the words twice. Circle the word that you hear twice. For example, if your teacher reads, "fit, pit, fit," you will circle the word *fit*.

pit	fit		pile	file
pig	fig		paint	faint
pail	fail		pat	fat
pour	four		peel	feel
pan	fan		pool	fool

Dictation

_____

_____

_____

_____

_____

_____

_____

Is there a special landmark in your district? Describe it and explain why you chose it. Is there a story about the landmark? Tell it to the class.

OR

Does your school or community have a memorial to anyone, or to any group of people? Read the inscription and find out why the memorial was made.

THE GOLDEN SWAN

Before You Read

- Answer the following questions.

  1. What does the title tell you? Do you think there could be a golden swan? Why or why not?
  2. What do you see in the illustration? What do you think is happening? How does the woman feel? Use your imagination. (There are no absolutely right answers to these questions.)

- Find Laos on the map at the front of the book. Then answer these questions.
  1. What is the country to the east of Laos?
  2. What is the country to the west of Laos?
  3. Where is Laos's border with China?
  4. Does Laos have a seacoast?
  5. What do you expect the climate to be?

Using What You Know

Do you know these words? If not, ask someone to help you with their meanings.

hunter	pale	grief	dream	widow
moonlight	gratitude	generous	depressed	gamble

here was once a mighty hunter who lived in Laos. He was a good husband and a kind father, and he looked after his family well. In fact, he was such a good hunter that people called him the Chief Hunter. People knew he was a very lucky man.

Everything about the Chief Hunter's life was fortunate. His children always had food. His wife could trade the birds and animals he caught for the best rice in the village. They had the best cloth to make their clothing. Life was rich and happy for the Chief Hunter's family.

Then one day the Chief Hunter hurt himself while he was hunting. He came home to his wife, and she said, "What is wrong? Your face is pale, and you are moving so slowly. What happened?"

"I don't know," the Chief Hunter said wearily. "I feel very sick. Let me lie down." So he took to his bed, and his family nursed him devotedly and watched him with great care.

At first the hunter seemed to get better, but then he slipped back. He died a week later.

His widow grieved terribly. She missed her husband, and she did not know how to live without him. The family became poor, and it was difficult to find enough food to eat. The children often cried when they went to sleep because they were hungry. The widow was at her wits' end. She could not sleep for worry and grief.

One night, as the poor widow tossed and turned in her sleep, she heard her husband's voice. "I have come back to help you," the voice said.

The widow sat up and looked around. She knew she was dreaming, and in her dream she went outside. A large swan spoke to her with the Chief Hunter's voice.

"I know how hard it is for you," the swan said in the Chief Hunter's voice.

The widow was happy to hear her husband's voice, yet sad because she knew it was a dream. Her throat closed so she could not speak. The swan stood in the moonlight and said, "I wish I could be here with you." Then it came closer. She could see that many of its feathers were made of gold. In the moonlight it seemed to be a golden swan.

The golden swan said, "Put your hand out and take one of my golden feathers. Use the money for food and clothing for yourself and the children. Go on. I will return whenever you need more. Pull a feather out of my wing." So, very gently, the widow pulled a feather out of the golden swan's wing.

The golden swan said in the voice of the Chief Hunter, "Go to sleep now. In the morning you will know that this was a special dream." So the widow put the feather beside her bed and went back to sleep. She slept so well and so deeply it was as if her man were still alive.

When she awoke, she remembered the dream and looked for the golden feather. There in its place was money and gold!

The wife wept with gratitude. Her husband was kind and generous even after death. Later she went to the village and bought food and clothing. She was careful not to spend too much. She was very quiet about her good fortune and decided to try to make the money last a long time.

She looked after the money well, but after a while there was very little left, and she began to worry. Would the golden swan come back again? On the day she spent the last coin, she felt alone again—just like when she was first a widow.

The golden swan came back to her, and she took a larger feather than before. The golden swan flew away, and the widow dreamed on and planned what she could do with the money.

The next day, sure enough, there was an even larger pile of gold and coins. The widow laughed and gave her children a little money to buy food in the market. Then she went to find the people who ran the gambling in the village. She was sure she could double her money.

"I would like to gamble," she said. "Will anyone play with me?"

"Do you have any money?" the gamblers asked.

"I have money," the widow said, and she let the gamblers see part of the gold.

The game started that morning, and by nightfall the widow had no money left. She went home, angry and depressed. On the way she thought of a plan.

"My husband will be angry when he finds out how I lost the money," she thought. "If I had a lot of money, I would not need to ask him for more."

That night as she lay down, she waited for the golden swan to come. He came as usual and offered his feathers. This time she plucked all the golden feathers she could find. She did not care how much she hurt the swan. She was possessed by greed. The widow put the feathers into a pile by her bed so that she could see them as soon as she woke up. "Such a large pile of feathers should turn into a lot of money," she thought.

The next morning she woke up and looked for the money. All she found was a pile of dull, dead swan's feathers.

That night the widow was afraid to go to sleep, but at last she did. The golden swan came to her in her dream and said, "I will never come to help you again. You do not deserve anything from me, and from now on you must look after yourself." Then the swan flew away and never returned. ▲

Understanding What You Read

Work with your partner and try to remember the story. (You can look back over the story if you like.) Which part did your partner like best?

Vocabulary

Write words and phrases from the story that have the same meaning as the underlined words and phrases.

1. He went to bed and stayed there. _____

2. His family looked after him very well while he was sick. _____

   _____

3. The hunter got worse. _____

4. The widow didn't know what to think or do. _____

   _____

5. One night the widow was sleeping restlessly. _____

   _____

6. The widow cried because she was grateful. _____

   _____

7. She was very greedy. _____

Discussion and Writing

1. The beginning of the story lists some things that made the Chief Hunter's family fortunate: he was a good husband and a kind father; and his family had enough to eat, good rice, and clothing. What things do you need to be happy? Talk to some other people and ask them to tell you five things that make them happy. Compare your list with your classmates.

2. Find evidence in the story that shows the character of the widow. How do you feel about her? Can you understand what she did?

3. What do you think the storytellers wanted people to learn from this story?

4. The beginning of the last paragraph says, "That night the widow was afraid to go to sleep, but at last she did." Why was she afraid? What could happen? Talk to your classmates and write down what the other people in your group suggest here.

Tell It Your Way

1. Work in groups. Write a summary of the story (between 100 and 150 words).
2. Do you know any stories like this one? If so, tell the story to your partner or the class.
3. "Then she went to find the people who ran the gambling in the village." Make up a play about the widow's gambling. Do you think the other gamblers felt sorry for her? What will they say when they see that she has money? What will they say when she has lost all her money?

Outside the Story

Ask people who are older than you what they need to make them happy. Write a report to share with the class. How do the things they say they need differ from the things you need? How are they the same?

Listening: Which Word Did You Hear Twice?

Many words in English have just one sound that makes them different from another word. Below you will find a list of words with just one sound difference. Your teacher will read the words to you, repeating one of the words twice. Circle the word that you hear twice. For example, if your teacher reads, "bid, bed, bid," you will circle the word *bid*.

bid	bed
did	dead
hid	head

pig	peg
chick	check
bill	bell
pin	pen
bit	bet
tin	ten
sit	set

Dictation

_____

_____

_____

_____

_____

_____

_____

_____

THE ELVES HELP AN OLD MAN

Before You Read

- Answer the following questions.

    1. What do you expect elves to look like?
    2. What do you see in the illustration? (There are no absolutely right answers to this question.)

- Find Japan on the map at the front of the book.

    1. Name two countries that are close to the biggest island of Japan.
    2. What is the name of the sea to the west of Japan?
    3. Which ocean is Japan in?
    4. Do you think Japan is as hot as Thailand? Explain your answer.
    5. In the story, you will read ". . . the night passed, and the sky became light in the east." Why is this so?

Using What You Know

Underline the words that relate to dancing. Be ready to explain why you chose the words you underlined.

swelling	medicine	thunder	steps	bow to somebody
jump	plan	elf	jig	rest
lightly	run	hop	sing	rhythm
music	waltz	jive	disco	wind
hollow	fiddle	square dance		

What other words relate to dancing?

33

nce upon a time in old Japan there was a man who had a growth on his face. It was a swelling in his cheek, and it made him look and feel ugly. The swelling was small when he was a young man, and then it began to grow. By the time of our story it was about the size of half a golf ball.

The old man did everything within his power to get rid of the swelling. He tried medicines, which he swallowed. He tried potions and ointments, which he rubbed on his face. He even thought of having the swelling cut off, but it was too dangerous. At last he decided that he must live with the swelling forever, and he tried to forget about it.

The old man's friends never understood how much the swelling worried him. It was not the first thing they thought about when they talked about him. They liked him because he was friendly, and generous, and he liked to dance. They liked to be with the old man, because he was fun. He had the gift of making other people happy.

One evening, as the old man returned home from the forest, a storm started. The thunder and lightning were terrifying, and the old man hid in a hollow tree.

"The storm has to pass soon," he thought to himself. The wind screamed past his tree, and it seemed as though the whole forest must fall. The old man hid himself deeper in the tree. "The weather is so bad that it simply has to end quickly," he told himself again. But still the wind blew and the trees shook.

The storm built up to a terrible noise, and then there was total silence. The old man listened, but he could hear nothing. "Am I deaf?" he wondered. "First, there was a din. Now there is no sound at all." He was about to get out of his hollow tree to see what had happened when he heard footsteps.

A large group of elves was coming toward him. The old man shrank back into his hiding place. They were the ugliest creatures anyone could possibly think of, and they were coming straight toward his tree.

The old man was terrified. He cowered in the dark and heard the elves touch the tree.

"This is the place," one said, and all the others agreed. They settled down under the tree and brought out a huge feast. The old man could smell the good food the elves were eating. They laughed and sang, they ate and drank, and the old man stayed as still as a stone.

After some time the elves became merry, and their singing grew louder. Some of them began to dance, and the others clapped and cheered. The old man crept up to watch them.

"I've seen many things," he said to himself, "but nothing like this! These elves love to dance, but they really aren't very good. They just do the same movements over and over. I can dance a lot better than they can." The old man moved carefully along a branch to see better.

More elves joined the dance, but their leader stayed on the ground, sitting with his back to the tree.

"I'm rather bored by your steps," the chief elf yawned. "Doesn't anyone know any other dances?"

Without thinking first, the old man replied, "I do."

"Who said that?" asked the elves. They looked up the tree and saw the old man. He had nowhere to hide, so he jumped down quickly.

"Do you know any new dances?" the chief elf asked.

"Of course," the old man said. "I've loved to dance since I was a boy. May I show you some steps?"

"Please do," the chief elf said.

The old man bowed low, and began to dance. "I must make them happy," he thought. "If I don't please them, they will probably kill me."

He danced as well as he possibly could. Some of the elves joined in, and he taught them his steps. He laughed to himself, for he truly loved to dance; and although he was an old man, his feet moved lightly enough.

The chief elf stopped the dancing. "Enough!" he cried. "This old man puts us all to shame. He dances better than any elf. But we must let him rest and eat and drink with us."

The elves gathered around the old man and offered him food and wine.

"I wonder what they plan to do to me?" the old man thought. "Who knows? I might as well enjoy the good things they offer me." So he ate and drank, and after a little while he got up again and danced some more. And so the night passed, and the sky became light in the east.

The chief elf said, "We want you to come back and dance with us again. We meet again tomorrow night." He called his advisers to him and said, "How can we be sure that he will return?"

A small elf said, "He has a swelling on his face. People on earth believe them to be valuable. He'll come back if we have that."

"Very clever," said the chief elf approvingly. Then the chief elf went to the old man and took the swelling off his face and handed it to the small elf. The small elf put the swelling into a bag to keep it safe.

The old man was amazed. He felt no pain at all, but the swelling was gone! He bowed low and departed quickly. He was so excited he could not walk. He ran and hopped and sang all the way home.

His wife was very glad to see him. "I've been so worried," she said. Then she looked again at his face. "What has happened?" she asked.

The old man told her the whole story, and she cried with pleasure, for she knew how much he hated that swelling. Then a neighbor came by, and the old man told him the story. In less than no time everyone in the little town knew about the old man's great good luck.

The old man's next door neighbor heard the story with great interest, for he had a swelling on his face, too. He listened carefully while the old man described exactly where the tree was.

"Why should he have all the luck?" the neighbor thought. "He has always been more fortunate than I am. He has a bigger house, and he has more friends than I do. However, that doesn't matter anymore. I can be as lucky as he is. He's even told me how!"

That night the neighbor crept out to find the tree. He climbed into the hollow and waited. Sure enough, after a while the troop of elves arrived. They were so ugly the poor neighbor was afraid and stayed hidden in the tree. He wanted to lose the swelling from his face, so he knew he must get down sometime.

Then the elves began to dance, and the neighbor jumped down from the tree and joined in.

"He's come back!" the small elf said.

"He isn't dancing very well tonight," another elf remarked.

The neighbor was a very bad dancer. He had no music in him. He flapped his arms, and he kicked his legs, and he jumped up and down, but nobody could say he danced. The elves tried to follow him but the old man became bad-tempered and told them they were clumsy and stupid.

The chief elf could stand no more. "Stop!" he commanded. "You came back, as we asked, and now we will let you go."

The small elf ran up with a bag, and the chief elf put his hand in and took out the old man's swelling.

"This is yours," he said, and put it on the neighbor's face.

And so the poor man crept to town with two swellings, one on each side of his face. ▲

Understanding What You Read

Circle the words that best complete the sentences.

There was once an old man who had a large (1. handsome, ugly, noisy) swelling on his face. One night he was coming home when he was caught in a storm and had to (2. live, eat, hide) in a hollow tree. After a while some (3. friends, neighbors, elves) came to dance under his tree. The old man taught the elves some new dances. They took the swelling off his face, because they wanted him to (4. go out, come back, run up) the next night. He was very happy indeed, and he (5. hurried, crept, walked) home to tell his wife and friends.

One of the old man's (6. neighbors, friends, relatives) also had a swelling on the side of his face. The neighbor went into the (7. forest, town, house) and found the elves, but he danced very badly. The elves gave him the first old man's (8. wife, swelling, dances) as well as his own.

Vocabulary

• Read the sentences. Circle the letter of the correct meaning for the underlined words. Use the meaning from the story.

1. The old man did everything <u>within his power</u> to get rid of the swelling.
   a. he was able to do
   b. with all his strength
   c. inside himself

2. First, there was a <u>din</u>.
   a. quietness
   b. absolute silence
   c. a loud noise

3. The old man <u>cowered</u> in the dark and heard the elves touch the tree.
   a. hid very carefully
   b. made a noise
   c. looked out

4. "<u>I'm rather bored by your steps</u>," the chief elf said.
   a. Your steps are very interesting to me
   b. One of your steps is dull
   c. Your steps are not interesting to me

5. This old man <u>puts us all to shame</u>.
   a. shows that we dance better than he does
   b. shows that we dance worse than he does
   c. shows us to be guilty

6. <u>In less than no time</u> everyone in the little town knew.
   a. After a long time
   b. Very soon
   c. Very slowly and steadily

7. <u>He flapped his arms</u>.
   a. He moved his arms around rhythmically
   b. He raised and lowered his arms gently
   c. He waved his arms about without rhythm

- Look back through the story to find out about the man who could dance well. Then write a description of him. Say what sort of old man he was.

Discussion and Writing

- Find out what these proverbs mean in English.

  1. Beauty is only skin deep.
  2. Handsome is as handsome does.
  3. You can't judge a book by its cover.
  4. Beauty is in the eye of the beholder.

  Do you have similar proverbs in your first language? Tell them to the class, and explain what they mean.

- Imagine a world in which everyone looks the same. What would the problems be in this world? Talk to your classmates, and then write a story beginning with this line: Everyone in the whole world looked exactly like everyone else.

Tell It Your Way

1. Do you know any stories like this one? If so, tell the story to your partner or to the class.
2. Pretend you are one of the elves. Tell your story to the class.

Outside the Story

Library Work

Find out more about elves. How do they differ from culture to culture, or country to country?

Listening: Which Word Did You Hear Twice?

Many words in English have just one sound that makes them different from another word. Below you will find a list of words with just one sound difference. Your teacher will read the words to you, repeating one of the words twice. Circle the word that you hear twice. For example, if your teacher reads, "than, Dan, than," you will circle the word *Dan*.

than	Dan	those	doze
there	dare	den	then
day	they	though	dough

Haiku

Haiku is a form of poetry written in Japan. There are three lines in the poem: the first one is short, the second long, and the third short. (Actually, Haiku are written with five syllables in the first line, seven in the second and five in the third, but we don't have to follow this rule absolutely.)

Choose one of the following subjects and think of as many words as you can that relate to it.

mother	water	dogs	old age	youth summer	
hunger	food	school	teachers	students	babies

Then write your haiku with a short first line, a longer second line, and a short third line. Here's an example:

A watching mother

Sees her child sleeping, dreaming

Blesses the night.

THE STORY OF WHITE ONION AND RED ONION

Before You Read

- Answer the following questions.

    1. What is a stepchild? a stepmother? a stepsister?
    2. What do you see in the illustration? (There are no absolutely right answers to this question.)

- Find Indonesia on the map at the front of the book. Check to see if you agree with these statements and then answer the questions that follow. Explain the reasons for your answers.

There are hundreds of small islands making up the country of Indonesia, the biggest of which is Java. Countries nearby include the Philippines, Malaysia, Singapore and Australia. Indonesia has a hot, steamy climate; rich, fertile soil; and some active volcanoes. There is a wet and a dry season, but no real winter and summer.

1. What sort of food do you think will grow well in Indonesia?
2. Do you expect the Indonesians to know a lot about sailing? Why?
3. What sort of clothes would be comfortable in Indonesia?

Using What You Know

Do you know the story of Cinderella? Give examples of the way Cinderella's stepmother treated Cinderella. How did the Fairy Godmother help Cinderella?

his is a story from Indonesia about a girl called White Onion. White Onion's mother died, and her father married another woman, who became White Onion's stepmother. White Onion's stepmother had a daughter of her own, called Red Onion, so Red Onion was White Onion's stepsister.

White Onion's stepmother loved her own daughter, Red Onion, but she was often unkind to White Onion. Then White Onion's father died, and there was nobody to protect her.

White Onion's stepmother saw her chance. "You eat too much," she told White Onion in a hard voice. "It costs a lot of money to look after you. From now on, you must work for your living." Then White Onion's stepmother called Red Onion and said gently, "Come, my darling, we're going out."

Red Onion looked pleased. She loved to go to the market. She wondered what they would buy.

"This is what you must do before I get back," White Onion's stepmother said to White Onion. "Sweep the house and get the dust out of all the corners. Then you must wash all the dirty clothes. And when we get home, have a meal ready."

"I can't do all that . . ." White Onion began to say, but it was too late. Her stepmother and Red Onion were walking away.

White Onion began to sweep the house. It was very dirty, so it took her a long time. The sun was low in the sky when she swept the last room.

She prepared the rice so that it was ready to cook, and she started cutting up the meat and vegetables for dinner. It was quite dark, and she was working as quickly as she could. "I do hope Red Onion and my stepmother are late," White Onion thought.

Red Onion and her mother arrived home a few minutes later. "Where's the meal?" Red Onion complained. "I'm tired and hungry after all the things we did today. You are lazy, White Onion. All you had to do was cook for us."

White Onion's stepmother returned with the broom. "You're a stupid, untidy girl," she said angrily. "This broom was lying where anyone could fall over it." She hit White Onion on the back. "This is to make you remember to be more careful. Now hurry up with our food."

"And be careful not to keep the best parts for yourself," said Red Onion.

The next day things were a little worse for White Onion, and the day after they were worse again. White Onion wished she could run away, but where could she go? Nobody was going to take her in. After a while White Onion began to believe what her stepmother told her. She thought she really was lazy and stupid.

So White Onion did all the hard work while Red Onion lived a life of ease. White Onion worked from dawn to dusk, cooking and sewing and sweeping. Doing the laundry in the river was her favorite task, for when she was at the river she was away from her stepmother's bitter tongue.

The river flowed quite quickly at the place where White Onion washed the clothes. One day she put her basket down on a rock. When she turned around, the basket was gone. It had been carried away by the water.

White Onion was terrified. She knew that her stepmother would beat her for losing the basket of clothes. "Perhaps I'll be able to find it," she thought. She ran along the side of the river, following the water downstream. She could not see her basket anywhere.

White Onion ran on and on, hoping to see the basket. She was tired and hungry and miserable, but still she went on. Finally she came around a bend in the river and met Mother Green Giant, who was the keeper of the river.

"Why are you here, my child?" the huge woman asked in a kind voice. White Onion looked up and saw Mother Green Giant looking at her in a comforting way.

"I lost my basket, Mother Green Giant," White Onion said shyly.

"Why is that so important?" Mother Green Giant asked.

So White Onion told her all about her life, and Mother Green Giant listened quietly. Then she handed White Onion a basket and said, "I believe this is yours. I found it in the river a little while ago."

White Onion was amazed. None of the clothes had fallen out of the basket!

"Thank you," White Onion said happily. "Thank you very much! I thought I had lost those clothes forever, and I hated to think what my stepmother would do. Thank you! Now I must hurry, for I have work to do." And she turned to go home.

"I would like you to come and work in my house for a few days," Mother Green Giant said. "Your stepmother will have to wait for a little while."

White Onion was glad to go with the giant, but she was horrified when she saw how big Mother Green Giant's house was. White Onion worked very hard, sweeping and cleaning the enormous rooms. As soon as she finished one room, she found another one that was even bigger. After three days of hard labor, the house was perfect. Mother Green Giant said it was time for her to go home.

"I want to give you a present, White Onion," Mother Green Giant said warmly. "I am very pleased with you. Now, come with me and choose any parcel you like."

Mother Green Giant led White Onion to a room full of packages. There were big, bright parcels tied up in silk, and small parcels tied with ribbons.

"Take any one you like," Mother Green Giant said. White Onion could not choose, so she quickly took a small parcel that was close to her. Then she thanked the giant and went home.

Red Onion and her mother were pleased to see White Onion. They had not liked looking after themselves. Now they had White Onion back to do the work.

"We thought you had drowned," Red Onion said.

"Where have you been?" White Onion's stepmother asked sharply.

White Onion explained what had happened. "Well, open the parcel," her stepmother said nastily. "Come on, child. I want to see what the giant would give to a nobody like you."

Slowly, White Onion started to unwrap the parcel. The middle of it was hard and lumpy under her fingers. She undid the last piece of paper and, to her astonishment, saw that it contained precious jewels. Her stepmother snatched them away. "I'm sure they're glass!" she said. White Onion looked at her angrily, and the stepmother handed the jewels back. "What a fool you were to take such a little package," she said.

Red Onion was furious at White Onion's good fortune. She decided to go to find Mother Green Giant and get a present for herself.

The next day, Red Onion took a basket of old clothes and dropped it into the river. Then she followed the basket downstream until she met Mother Green Giant. Red Onion was not used to walking, so she was hot and uncomfortable.

"Have you seen my basket?" Red Onion asked rudely.

"It's over there," the giant said, without even looking up from her washing.

Red Onion picked up her basket and said, "Can I work for you?"

Mother Green Giant sighed. "If you wish," she said, and she led Red Onion back to her enormous house.

Red Onion started to work, but she really didn't know how to clean the house. She was naturally clumsy, and she bumped into things and hurt herself. After a few hours, lazy Red Onion sat down and whined, "I want to go home. Can I have my present?"

Mother Green Giant took Red Onion to the room with all the parcels. Red Onion looked carefully at them all. She weighed them in her hand and shook them to see what was in them. After a while, the giant grew impatient and said sharply, "Hurry up, please. Take your gift and go."

Red Onion took the biggest and heaviest parcel she could find, and she set off to drag it home. She was nearly exhausted when she arrived. She said to White Onion, "Now you see what you should have chosen. Imagine how many jewels there are in *this* package!"

Red Onion and her mother started to undo the many knots that held the parcel together. They tore greedily at the beautiful wrappings until they got to a large box.

Red Onion and her mother pushed White Onion aside and lifted the lid. They saw two bright sparkling lights in the box. As they peered into the box, there was a hiss. They saw that the lights were the eyes of a snake.

Swiftly, the snake slid out of the box and bit the two women. Then it slithered past White Onion and disappeared. Nobody ever saw it again.

Red Onion collapsed at once, and her mother died a few minutes later. White Onion, however, stayed on in the house and lived there peacefully for the rest of her long and happy life. ▲

Understanding What You Read

Put these events in the correct order. Write 1 by the first event. Write 7 by the last event. The first one is done for you.

_____ 1. Mother Green Giant returned the basket to White Onion.

_____ 2. White Onion worked at Mother Green Giant's house.

_____ 3. The snake killed Red Onion and her mother.

_____ 4. Mother Green Giant gave White Onion a present.

_____ 5. Red Onion brought home the biggest parcel she could find.

_1_ 6. One day White Onion lost a basket of clothes in the river.

_____ 7. Red Onion wanted a present too.

Vocabulary

• Write words and phrases from the story that have the same meaning as the underlined words and phrases.

1. White Onion had nobody to underline{keep her safe}. _____
2. You must do work so that you underline{earn what you eat}. _____

3. She <u>didn't know for certain</u>. _____

4. Now <u>be quick</u> with our food. _____

5. Red Onion lived <u>a very easy life</u>. _____

6. <u>The person who looked after</u> the river. _____

7. "We thought you <u>had died under the water</u>." _____

8. The giant <u>became tired of waiting</u>. _____

9. As they <u>looked very carefully</u> into the box. _____

Tic-Tac-Toe

You should be in two teams. Team A has 30 seconds to choose a square and make up a sentence using the word in that square. Team B has 30 seconds to decide whether the sentence is correct and, if not, to correct it. The teacher will then put an A next to the word in the grid if the sentence was really correct. If it was wrong and Team B corrected it properly, the teacher will put a B next to the word. The first team to get three letters in a row, diagonally, vertically, or horizontally, wins.

sweeps	washed	cooking
carried	follow	work
clean	pushing	walks

Discussion and Writing

1. Why do people say this is a Cinderella story? Compare it with the story of Cinderella that you know. How are the stories similar? How are they different?

2. What do you think the story teaches people?

3. The underlined words and phrases in the following sentences tell how someone said something. Working with your partner, read aloud the parts of the sentences that are inside the quotation marks. Try to make your voice sound the way the story says.

   a. "You eat too much," the stepmother told White Onion <u>in a hard voice</u>.

   b. White Onion's stepmother returned with the broom. "You're a stupid, untidy girl," she said <u>angrily</u>.

   c. "Why are you here?" the huge woman asked <u>in a kind voice</u>.

   d. "I lost my basket," White Onion said <u>shyly</u>.

   e. "Thank you," White Onion said <u>happily</u>.

   f. "I want to give you a present, White Onion," Mother Green Giant said <u>warmly</u>.

   g. "Well, open the parcel," her stepmother said <u>nastily</u>.

   h. Mother Green Giant <u>sighed</u>. "If you wish," she said.

   i. After a few hours, lazy Red Onion sat down and <u>whined</u>, "I want to go home. Can I have my present?"

   j. After a while, the giant grew impatient and said <u>sharply</u>, "Hurry up, please. Take your gift and go."

Tell It Your Way

1. Do you know any stories like this one? If so, tell the story to your partner or the class.

2. Make another ending to this story. For example, the snake tells White Onion that Red Onion and the stepmother are her slaves . . .

3. Mime the following parts of the story.

   a. When Mother Green Giant meets White Onion, and White Onion works for her and takes her present.

   b. When Mother Green Giant meets Red Onion, and Red Onion works for her and takes her present.

   Be careful to move in a way that shows how Mother Green Giant feels about each of the young women.

Outside the Story

Library Work

1. Find other stories about giants. Are they all as kind as Mother Green Giant? Take one or two giants, and compare them with her.

2. Find out what you can about the tourist industry in Indonesia. What are the hotels like? What can you see there? Plan a visit to the country. Say where you will go and what you will see. What time of the year will you go? Why?

Listening: Which Word Did You Hear Twice?

Many words in English have just one sound that makes them different from another word. Below you will find a list of words with just one sound difference. Your teacher will read the words to you, repeating one of the words twice. Circle the word that you hear twice. For example, if your teacher reads, "fail, veil, fail," you will circle the word *fail*.

fail	veil	few	view
fan	van	fine	vine
fat	vat	final	vinyl
fault	vault	ferry	very
fast	vast		

Game: The Teacher's Cat

The first student makes up a sentence about the teacher's cat using an adjective beginning with A. (The teacher's cat is an awkward cat.) The second student makes up a sentence about the teacher's cat using a B, and so on through the alphabet. Students may use words beginning with ex, like excited or excellent, for the letter X. Students drop out if they

*   fail to use a word beginning with the correct letter
*   repeat a word already used
*   take longer than the time allowed to respond (usually ten seconds to begin with)
*   fail to think of a word.

THE ANIMALS OF THE CHINESE ZODIAC

Before You Read

- Answer the following questions.

    1. What do you know about astrology?
    2. Can the stars influence the way we behave? Can we tell the future?
    3. How much can we know about other people?
    4. What do you see in the illustrations?

Using What You Know

A lunar year is counted by the cycles of the moon, so it is not exactly the same as a calendar year. A calendar year lasts 365 days, 366 in a leap year. A leap year falls every four years, in a year divisible by four, like 1996. That's why February 29 comes every four years. Would you like your birthday to be on February 29? Why? Why not?

The lunar year is twelve months of approximately 29-1/2 days, or approximately 354-1/3 days. This means important festivals, like the Lunar New Year, fall on different dates each year.

1. Look at the following chart. Find out what animal sign controls the year you were born.

    For instance, if you were born between February 3, 1973, and January 23, 1974, you are an ox. If you were born between February 2, 1984, and February 19, 1985, you are a rat. Do not tell anybody what your sign is.

Forty Lunar Years from 1940 to 2000

February 8, 1940, to January 26, 1941: Dragon
January 27, 1941, to February 14, 1942: Snake
February 15, 1942, to February 3, 1943: Horse
February 4, 1943, to January 24, 1944: Goat
January 25, 1944, to February 11, 1945: Monkey
February 12, 1945, to February 1, 1946: Rooster
February 2, 1946, to January 21, 1947: Dog
January 22, 1947, to February 9, 1948: Pig
February 10, 1948, to January 28, 1949: Rat
January 29, 1949, to February 15, 1950: Ox
February 16, 1950, to February 5, 1951: Tiger
February 6, 1951, to January 25, 1952: Rabbit
January 26, 1952, to February 13, 1953: Dragon
February 14, 1953, to February 2, 1954: Snake
February 3, 1954, to January 23, 1955: Horse
January 24, 1955, to February 10, 1956: Goat
February 11, 1956, to January 29, 1957: Monkey
January 30, 1957, to February 17, 1958: Rooster
February 18, 1958, to February 6, 1959: Dog
February 7, 1959, to January 27, 1960: Pig
January 28, 1960, to February 14, 1961: Rat
February 15, 1961, to February 4, 1962: Ox
February 5, 1962, to January 24, 1963: Tiger
January 25, 1963, to February 12, 1964: Rabbit
February 13, 1964, to January 31, 1965: Dragon
February 1, 1965, to January 20, 1966: Snake

January 21, 1966, to February 8, 1967: Horse
February 9, 1967, to January 28, 1968: Goat
January 29, 1968, to February 15, 1969: Monkey
February 16, 1969, to February 5, 1970: Rooster
February 6, 1970, to January 25, 1971: Dog
January 26, 1971, to February 14, 1972: Pig
February 15, 1972, to February 2, 1973: Rat
February 3, 1973, to January 23, 1974: Ox
January 24, 1974, to February 10, 1975: Tiger
February 11, 1975, to January 30, 1976: Rabbit
January 31, 1976, to February 17, 1977: Dragon
February 18, 1977, to February 6, 1978: Snake
February 7, 1978, to January 27, 1979: Horse
January 28, 1979, to February 15, 1980: Goat
February 16, 1980, to February 4, 1981: Monkey
February 5, 1981, to January 24, 1982: Rooster
January 25, 1982, to February 12, 1983: Dog
February 13, 1983, to February 1, 1984: Pig
February 2, 1984, to February 19, 1985: Rat
February 20, 1985, to February 8, 1986: Ox
February 9, 1986, to January 28, 1987: Tiger
January 29, 1987, to February 16, 1988: Rabbit
February 17, 1988, to February 5, 1989: Dragon
February 6, 1989, to January 25, 1990: Snake
January 26, 1990, to February 13, 1991: Horse
February 14, 1991, to February 2, 1992: Goat
February 3, 1992, to January 21, 1993: Monkey
January 22, 1993, to February 9, 1994: Rooster
February 10, 1994, to January 30, 1995: Dog
January 31, 1995, to February 18, 1996: Pig
February 19, 1996, to February 6, 1997: Rat
February 7, 1997, to January 27, 1998: Ox
January 28, 1998, to February 15, 1999: Tiger
January 16, 1999, to February 4, 2000: Rabbit

2. While you are reading, try to guess which signs your classmates have.

The signs of the Chinese Zodiac go in this order: rat, ox, tiger, rabbit, dragon, snake, horse, goat, monkey, rooster, dog, and pig.

People born under the sign of the rat are energetic. They are always busy, and they don't often sit and think. Rats are charming people who try very hard to make other people like them. They usually seem peaceful, and they are very good at hiding how they really feel. They can be boiling with anger inside and still look calm.

Rats like to lead. They enjoy getting other people to do what they want them to do. Rats like to gamble, and they often play cards very well. They like to have a few good friends. They enjoy expensive places and can be very generous with people they are fond of.

People born under the sign of the ox are very sensible. They work hard and steadily to get what they want. They don't really like new ideas, and they don't like change. Oxen are very practical. They do not really enjoy poetry or things they can't understand immediately. Oxen are sometimes so busy working hard that they forget to play.

Tigers are nothing like oxen. They are brave and confident and believe they can do whatever they set out to do. They are also unpredictable, so you can never tell what they will do next! Tigers love to go to parties, and they are generous with their friends when they feel like it. A tiger will take a lot of risks in business. Tigers love to be free, and they find it hard to settle down in a marriage.

Rabbits are quiet, tactful creatures who try not to hurt other people's feelings. A rabbit is usually very clever and likes to do things correctly. Some people say that rabbits are perfectionists and cannot bear to make mistakes. If a rabbit does not like a person or an event, he or she will quietly go somewhere else. Rabbits like to live in a comfortable place, and they try to keep their home quiet and calm. They hate to argue and will try very hard to avoid disagreements.

The next year belongs to the dragon. Dragons are big, brave, bold people. You always notice them first because they stand out in a crowd. The dragon makes big plans for the future. In fact, dragons have major problems with details, and they often forget to check all the little things in a plan. Dragons are very truthful and honest, but sometimes they are too quick to tell the whole truth. A dragon says things like "I usually like soup, but this one you made is not very good."

The year of the snake follows the year of the dragon. Snakes are thinkers. They will consider a problem long after everyone else has stopped. Snakes are persevering. They keep on trying when other people have given up. Snakes love luxury. They like to wear good clothes, and they like to go to expensive places. It is not surprising that they also like to wear jewelry, and they enjoy eating the finest food.

Snakes have a problem with laziness. They do not like to work with their hands, but prefer to use their minds.

Those born in the year of the horse are extremely physically active. They love games and races, and they are friendly and entertaining. They love jokes, but they sometimes don't know when to stop. Horses are often very clever and have wonderful ideas. However, they are easily distracted. Unless you watch them carefully, they can leave things half done. They are very charming and find it easy to persuade their friends to do things. They make wonderful salespeople.

Goats are quiet and sincere, but they suffer from feelings of gloom. Goats spend a lot of time worrying about bad things that will probably not happen. They enjoy concerts and music, and you will often find them in art galleries. They like strange plays that are difficult to understand. Goats are not very concerned about making money, although they love to spend it on beautiful things. They are very creative, and they paint and write very well. Goats are usually lucky when they gamble. They enjoy a game of chance.

The year of the monkey comes next. People born in the year of the monkey are very intelligent and extremely active, although sometimes they look very quiet and shy. They love to bargain, and you should never forget how clever they are. They like to look their best and will spend a lot of money on clothes. Monkeys have extremely good memories, and they love to make people laugh. The monkey's weakness is a lack of persistence; they tend to give up easily.

Those born in the year of the rooster are complicated people who are difficult to understand. They love to show off what they can do, and they hate to admit mistakes. However, a rooster will happily tell other people what mistakes they have made and will criticize and advise freely. Roosters will forgive people who do them wrong, but they will not let the person who hurt them go without a long lecture. Roosters love to think hard about things. They enjoy detective stories and are very inquisitive.

The second to last year of the cycle is the year of the dog. People born in the year of the dog are kind, loyal friends who will stay with their friends through good times and bad. They will say what they think in a most tactless and outspoken way. However, there is a quiet side to the dog, and they secretly worry a lot. Dogs love to spend money. They are very honest and look after their friends' money well, but they are often careless with their own.

Our last sign is the pig. Those born under this sign are kind, friendly, and brave. They are very obliging and will do a great deal to help their friends. You can always rely on them and trust them to help you.

Pigs are very good with money, and they make good bankers and investors. They enjoy working to raise money for charity and other good causes. ▲

Understanding What You Read

Fill in the blanks in the following sentences. The first one has been done for you.

1. _Snakes_   are lazy and do not like to work with their hands.

2. _____ are quiet and hate arguments.

3. _____ love to play jokes and sometimes go too far!

4. _____ are very trustworthy and will help their friends.

5. _____ are tactless and outspoken and worry a lot.

6. _____ worry a lot and are very creative.

7. _____ do not like change or new things they do not understand.

8. _____ love to criticize and are very complicated.

9. _____ have big plans and no sense of detail.

10. _____ love to bargain, have good ideas, but tend to give up easily.

11. _____ are brave and enjoy taking risks.

12. _____ are energetic and charming and can hide how they feel.

Vocabulary

Complete the crossword puzzle. Use words from the story.

Across

  4. Someone who cares about others is _____.
  5. Someone who makes you like them is _____.
  8. Someone who enjoys making things is _____.
  9. Someone who is brave and noticeable is _____.
10. Something that costs a lot is _____.
11. Someone who is able to say things gently without making people angry is _____ .

Down

1. When you do something without changing pace, you do it _____.
2. To tell someone what to do is to _____ them.
3. If you believe you can do what you set out to do, you are _____.
6. _____ is another word for clever.
7. People who are busy and keep doing things are _____.

Discussion

Go around the class and find out what sign your classmates have. When you find out, fill in the chart below. We did an example for you.

Student	Sign	True because	False because
Mei Ling	monkey	intelligent and active	She is very persistent!

Tell It Your Way

1. Do you believe in astrology? Why? Why not?

2. When you find out somebody's animal sign, you know what year they were born and how old they are. Is it polite to ask somebody how old they are in your country? Is it polite in the United States? Work with your classmates and find out if there are any questions that are polite in one country and not another. Make a list below.

3. What do these animals stand for in your culture?

rat	ox	tiger	rabbit	dragon	snake
horse	goat	monkey	rooster	dog	pig

Outside the Story

Get a copy of the astrological forecast from a newspaper or magazine. Look at the prediction for your sign and interpret it relating to your life. Find other people with the same sign. What does the prediction mean for them? How can one message be interpreted so many ways?

Birds of a Feather Flock Together, or Opposites Attract

Consider your sign in the Chinese Zodiac and look at the characteristics of the other signs. Which signs could you marry? Why?

Listening: Which Word Did You Hear Twice?

Many words in English have just one sound that makes them different from another word. Below you will find a list of words with just one sound difference. Your teacher will read the words to you, repeating one of the words twice. Circle the word that you hear twice. For example, if your teacher reads, "bed, bad, bad," you will circle the word *bad*.

bed	bad		send	sand
head	had		beg	bag
said	sad		leg	lag
end	and		bet	bat
met	mat		set	sat

THE WOODCUTTER IN THE MOON

Before You Read

- Answer the following questions.

    1. What other words do you think of when you think of a cruel person? How do you expect a cruel person to behave?
    2. What do you see in the illustration? (There are no absolutely right answers to this question.)

- Find China on the map at the front of the book. Then answer these questions.

    1. How big is China compared to the other countries in Asia?
    2. What do you think the climate is like in the north of China?
    3. What do you think the climate is like in the south of China?
    4. The story is about someone who is punished in a very cold place. Do you think the story began in the north of China or the south?

Using What You Know

1. What do all these words have in common?

   swallow   hen   rooster   cock   sparrow
   swan   peck   twitter   fly   hop

2. Circle the words that have something to do with being surprised.

   wounded   amazed   astonished   dazzled   excited

here was once a very kind young man who lived in old China. One day he found a wounded swallow in the road and took it home with him. He brought it food and water and nursed it tenderly until it recovered. The young man became very fond of the bird. However, he knew that when the bird was well, it was time to let it go.

The young man took the bird to the window so that it could see the outside world. It hopped about on the windowsill and flew away. But then, to his great joy, it flew back to him. The next day he took it to the window again, and it flew out and around the garden. He watched it anxiously, but once again the bird returned to the room. On the third day, however, the bird flew out of the window and away into the sky.

The young man was very sad. He missed the swallow's company. He looked out of his window one day at the empty sky. "I wonder how the swallow is faring," he thought, and came back inside.

There was a twittering at the window, and the young man saw the bird had come back. It stood on the window sill with a large seed in its beak. Then it put the seed down, gave a little bow, and flew away.

The young man took the bird's gift in his hand. He planted the seed in the garden and cared for it well. The seed sprouted at once, and he was amazed to see the way the plant grew. Within days he had a large pumpkin vine, which bore just one enormous pumpkin. When it was ripe, he opened it and was astonished to find that it was full of gold and silver.

People heard about the young man's good fortune and came to praise him for his kindness. The story of the wounded bird spread far and wide, and another young man decided he would make himself lucky too.

This cruel young man crept up on a swallow that was sitting on a fence. He knocked it to the ground. Then he took the injured bird home, looked after it, and nursed it back to health. He released it when it was better. To his great delight, the bird brought him a pumpkin seed. He planted the seed, and a pumpkin grew almost immediately. It was the largest pumpkin he had ever seen, and the young man waited patiently. Every day he looked at it and tried to guess how much gold it would contain. At last it was ripe, and the young man prepared to open it. He was extremely excited.

The young man carefully sliced the pumpkin open. To his great surprise, a well dressed old man stepped out of the vegetable. "You are a wicked person," the old man said calmly. "You worship gold, and now I am going to take you to where there is more wealth than you can imagine." The old man took the young man's arm and stepped onto the pumpkin vine.

The pumpkin vine turned into a ladder and rose to the sky, carrying them with it. The bottom rungs of the ladder fell away, so it was impossible to go back down. The young man saw that they were flying toward the moon.

The vine ladder stopped on the moon outside the Palace of Boundless Cold. The moon was frozen, but the young man saw nothing but the dazzling brilliance of the place. The roads were made of jade set with precious stones. Inside the palace there were glittering gems set in gold. They gave off so much light that he could not bear to keep his eyes open. The young man wandered about, stunned by what he saw, unable to think or act.

At last he asked the old man to let him return to earth. "Of course," the old man replied, "but you must perform a task first. You must cut down this cinnamon tree." And he gave the young man a silver ax.

The cinnamon tree was made of gold and set with precious jewels. "If I can take this tree back to earth, I shall be rich forever," the young man thought, and he set to work with a will. As he made the first cut on the trunk of the tree, he felt a sharp pain in his shoulders. He looked around to see a silver white cock and turned to drive it away. When he looked back, the cut in the tree had healed as though he had never touched it.

He tried to cut the tree again. The rooster struck him, and the wood of the tree grew back together again. He swung the ax again, the rooster pecked him, and the wood grew back again. And so it is to this day. When you look into the moon, you can see the cruel young man still trying to cut down the tree. His task goes on forever, and he will never come back home to the warmth of the earth. ▲

Understanding What You Read

Complete the story by filling in the gaps below.

A kind young man found a sick swallow and _____
                                                          A
_____. When the bird got better, the young man

_____, but the bird flew back again. At last the
              B
bird gave the young man a _____ and flew away forever. When
                                        C
the kind young man planted the seed, it grew into _____
                                                              D
_____ full of gold and silver.

Another young man heard the story. He _____ a bird
E
and then nursed it back to health. The bird gave him a seed, which grew
into a pumpkin vine with one big pumpkin. When the young man opened
it, _____ and took him to the moon. The old
F
man said that he could go back to earth when _____
G
_____ . Every time he cut the tree with the ax

_____ .
H

Vocabulary

Match the following words (1–7) with their meanings (a–g). The first one has
been done for you.

_e_	1. wounded	a.	luck
_____	2. fortune	b.	evil
_____	3. sliced	c.	without limit
_____	4. wicked	d.	do
_____	5. ladder	e.	hurt
_____	6. boundless	f.	something you use to climb
_____	7. perform	g.	cut

Tic-Tac-Toe

You should be in two teams. Team A has 30 seconds to choose a square and
make up a sentence using the word in that square. Team B has 30 seconds to
decide whether the sentence is correct and, if not, to correct it. The teacher will
then put an A next to the word in the grid if the sentence was really correct. If
it was wrong, and Team B corrected it properly, the teacher will put a B next to
the word. The first team to get three letters in a row, diagonally, vertically, or
horizontally, wins.

nursed	hopped	praised
wandered	healed	sprouted
stepped	flew	watched

Discussion and Writing

The Five Senses: How Ideas Can Fit Together

1. Work with a classmate, and answer the following questions. Be prepared to explain your choices to the rest of the class. (There are no absolutely right or wrong answers.)

   Here is an example of what one student wrote for quietness.

What would quietness sound like?	*a gentle hum*
What color would quietness be?	*pale gray*
What would quietness taste like?	*vanilla ice cream*
What would quietness smell like?	*an old library*
What would quietness feel like?	*soft velvet*

   What would kindness sound like?

   What color would kindness be?

   What would kindness taste like?

   What would kindness smell like?

   What would kindness feel like?

   What would cold sound like?

   What color would cold be?

   What would cold taste like?

   What would cold smell like?

   What does cold feel like?

2. Work with a partner and compare the behavior of the kind young man with that of the cruel young man. Did the woodcutter deserve such a terrible punishment? Be ready to explain your answer.

kind young man	cruel young man

OR

Work with a partner and describe how the cruel young man feels when he looks back at the earth. Do you feel sorry for him? Explain your answer.

Tell It Your Way

Draw the different parts of the story on the chalkboard. With your classmates, decide how many different pictures you will need.

Outside the Story

Library Work

Find out about King Sisyphus. What was his task? What does his story have in common with the story of the woodcutter in the moon?

Listening: Which Word Did You Hear Twice?

Many words in English have just one sound that makes them different from another word. Below you will find a list of words with just one sound difference. Your teacher will read the words to you, repeating one of the words twice. Circle the word that you hear twice. For example, if your teacher reads, "bed, bud, bud," you will circle the word *bud*.

bed	bud	leg	lug
bled	blood	bet	but
end	and	rest	rust
bug	beg	desk	dusk
deck	duck	pep	pup

Dictation

_____

_____

_____

_____

_____

_____

_____

_____

THE FLYING FAIRY WIFE

Before You Read

- Answer the following questions.

    1. What does the title mean?
    2. What do you see in the illustration?

- Find Korea on the map at the front of the book. Then answer these questions.

    1. What country is to the north and west of Korea?
    2. Where is Japan in relation to Korea?
    3. What is the name of the sea in Korea's eastern coastline?
    4. What ocean is it in?
    5. What is a land mass like Korea called?

Using What You Know

Find the meaning for each word. Then write the letters of the correct meaning on the line. The first one has been done for you.

<u>c</u>   1. long for   a. hurt

____ 2. handsome   b. place where a river falls over rocks

____ 3. filthy   c. want very badly

____ 4. bathe   d. very dirty

____ 5. wounded   e. wash one's body

____ 6. waterfall   f. good looking

nce upon a time, in old Korea, there lived a very poor young woodcutter. He lived alone in his tiny hut in the forest and longed for a wife. He wanted very much to have someone to come home to in the evenings. But he was sad, because he had very little to offer to a wife. He did not think he was very handsome, and he had very little money. So he quietly cut wood and sold it in the market, and he lived alone.

One day he was out in the forest when he heard the noise of a hunt. A wounded deer burst through the bushes near him and said, "Please help me! The hunters have shot me already. See! I am hurt! If they catch me they'll kill me."

Quickly the woodcutter led the deer to his hut and hid it. Then he went back to work as though nothing had happened. A few minutes later he saw the hunters go past. When they were far away, he went back to his hut.

"I want to repay you," the deer said. "I think you need a wife."

The woodcutter nodded.

"I know where you can find one," the deer said. "Do you know where the river goes over the rocks at Nine Dragon Falls?"

The hunter replied that he knew the waterfalls. There were eight pools of water there.

"Go to the pools," the deer said, "and wait for the fairy princesses of heaven to fly down to bathe in them. The princesses leave their dresses by the side of the pool. Choose your favorite, and steal her clothes. She can't fly home without her magic dress. You can ask her to be your wife. When you are married, be sure you have three children before you let her see her dress. If she has only two children, she can put the dress on and fly back to heaven with a baby under each arm. If she has three children, she will not be able to carry them all." Before the woodcutter could ask any questions the deer bounded away.

The very next day the woodcutter went to Nine Dragon Falls and waited. Sure enough, the princesses flew down from heaven to bathe. He stole the clothes that belonged to the youngest, so she could not leave.

All the sisters searched for the missing dress, but at last they had to go back to heaven. They left the youngest sister behind, crying bitterly.

The woodcutter crept out from where he had been hiding. "Please don't cry," he said gently. "I'll look after you, I promise. I'll work very hard and cut a lot of wood, and we'll be happy."

At first the princess was very frightened. Then she looked at the woodcutter, and she saw a handsome young man with a kind face. He talked to her gently, and she began to feel better. At last she agreed to stay with the woodcutter and be his wife. The woodcutter was very happy, and he carefully hid the dress where the princess could never find it.

Even after she was married, the poor princess went every day to the pool to look for her sisters, but they never came back. After a while she grew to like being on earth, and she came to love the woodcutter.

And so the years passed, and they had two children, a boy and a girl. The woodcutter, who loved his wife dearly, began to feel sorry that he had tricked her. One fateful day he showed her the magic dress.

Her face changed as she looked at it. "Where did you get this?" she asked angrily.

"I stole it from Nine Dragon Falls," the woodcutter confessed.

"I have been so homesick," she cried angrily, "and you have let me endure the pain for all these years! Now I can go home." Before the woodcutter could stop her, she put the dress on, took their two children, and flew away.

The woodcutter wanted to die. He stayed in his hut and wept for his wife and children. He did not go to work, and he let the hut get filthy. Life had no joy for him.

One night the deer spoke to him in a dream. "I can tell you how to get back to your family," the deer said. "Go to Nine Dragon Falls. The princesses do not bathe there any more. Instead they send down a silver bucket to carry water into the sky. Climb into the bucket, and they will pull you up to heaven."

So the woodcutter did as the deer said and waited by the waterfall. At midday he saw a silver bucket coming down to the water. He climbed in, and he felt the bucket rising into the sky. He was glad to leave the earth to be with his family.

His wife waited in the heavens, very happy to see the woodcutter rising toward her. People say that you can see the woodcutter and his wife among the stars. They are happy to be together again at last. ▲

Understanding What You Read

Put the following events in the story in the correct order.

_____ 1. The fairy wife flew back to heaven.

_____ 2. The deer told the woodcutter how to find his family in heaven.

_____ 3. The woodcutter stole the youngest fairy's dress.

_____ 4. The woodcutter showed his fairy wife her magic dress.

_____ 5. The woodcutter saved a deer from the hunters.

_____ 6. The deer told the woodcutter where the fairies bathed.

Vocabulary

Read the sentences. Circle the letter of the correct meaning for the underlined words. Use the meaning from the story.

1. But he was sad, because he had very little to offer.
   a. to give
   b. to use
   c. to take

2. The deer was afraid the hunters would kill it.
   a. people who were chasing it
   b. animals that were chasing it
   c. both animals and people who were chasing it

3. I want to repay you.
   a. give money to you
   b. do something cruel to you
   c. do something for you because you helped me

4. Choose your favorite, and steal her clothes.
   a. the one you like the least
   b. the one you like best
   c. the youngest one

5. "I stole it from Nine Dragon Falls," the woodcutter confessed.
   a. admitted
   b. said happily
   c. laughed

6. "I have <u>been so homesick</u>," she cried.
   a. been so sick at home
   b. left home so often
   c. missed my home so much

Discussion and Writing

1. How do you think the fairy princess felt when she could not find her clothes? Years later, when she discovered her husband had stolen them?

   Work with a friend, and describe her emotions. Talk about what she thought and about how her body felt.

2. What sort of person was the woodcutter? Go back through the story and look for things he did. Then write a description of him below. The first one has been done for you.

   a. We know the woodcutter was modest, because ____*he did not*____ *believe he was very handsome.*_____

   b. We know the woodcutter was lonely, because _____
   _____

   c. We know the woodcutter was kind, because _____
   _____

   d. We know the woodcutter loved his wife, because _____
   _____

Tell It Your Way

1. Pretend you are the woodcutter's fairy princess wife. Tell your story to the class.

2. Make up an advertisement for the fairy princess's lost dress.

3. Act out the following parts of the story without speaking.

   a. When the fairy princess is looking for her dress
   b. When the princess finds out her husband stole her magic dress

4. Do you know any other stories like this one? If so, tell the story to your partner or to the class. Where did you hear your story?

Outside the Story

People have always wanted to fly like birds. Go to the library and read about Icarus. Tell his story to the class.

Game

Write a sentence about flying on a piece of paper and pass it to the person next to you. That person reads your sentence, adds another sentence, and passes it on to the next person. The last person hands the piece of paper back to you, and you read the whole passage.

Listening: Which Word Did You Hear Twice?

Many words in English have just one sound that makes them different from another word. Below you will find a list of words with just one sound difference. Your teacher will read the words to you, repeating one of the words twice. Circle the word that you hear twice. For example, if your teacher reads, "sack, shack, sack," you will circle the word *sack*.

sack	shack	self	shelf
said	shed	sell	shell
same	shame	sip	ship
see	she	sort	short
seed	she'd	sue	shoe

Dictation

_____

_____

_____

_____

_____

_____

_____

THE LEGEND OF MAGDAPIO

Before You Read

- Answer the following question.

    1. What do you see in the illustration?

- Find the Philippines on the map at the front of the book and name the countries that are its neighbors. Which countries do you expect the people of the Philippines to visit the most? How would stories travel?

Using What You Know

Have you heard the story of Romeo and Juliet? What did the lovers want to do? What did their families do? How did it all end?

agda was born into a loving family. When she was a little girl her parents played with her. Her mother and grandmother taught her to sing and took her swimming in the river. There was no happier child, and Magda grew up with a sunny disposition and a heart full of joy. Her parents felt that she was a special little girl, and they watched her devotedly.

As Magda grew up, her family began to think about the sort of man she should marry. This man must be brave, good, strong, and kind. He must be a great hunter. He must come from a good family. He must be all things to all men. The family dreamed of a perfect man who could not possibly exist in the real world.

Magda, however, had already found a young man whom she loved. His name was Pio. He was good and kind, but he was not the ideal man that her family wanted.

Pio loved Magda in return. Whenever he saw her, his heart jumped, and he felt very happy. He wanted very much to marry Magda and to be with her constantly and forever.

Magda said, "Let me talk quietly to my family. Let me see what they say when I tell them that I'm in love. Perhaps they'll understand." But in her heart she knew that it was very unlikely that her family would agree to her marrying an ordinary young man like Pio. She had never seen the other members of Pio's family, which was strange. She knew everyone else for miles around.

She spoke first to her grandmother. "I think I've found the man I want to marry," she told the old woman.

Her grandmother looked surprised. "Who is it?" she asked. "What is he like?"

"He's kind and honest . . ." Magda began.

"Tell me who he is," her grandmother interrupted.

"It's Pio," Magda replied.

"Pio! Pio!" The grandmother thought hard, but she couldn't think of anyone called Pio. And then she remembered him: a quiet boy, ordinary, and no match for her wonderful Magda. He was a member of a family that had argued and fought with Magda's for as long as anyone could remember.

"I think you should talk to your parents," the old woman said. "Perhaps they know a lot more about Pio than I do."

Magda's parents were not pleased. "He's not a bad young man," her father said, "but he's not the sort of husband we want for you, my dear. Our families have tried to stay away from each other, and for good reason. Now run on. I shall call some of the finest young men to the village, and we will arrange a marriage for you."

Magda went away quietly, resolved to wait until her parents changed their minds. She knew that no matter how she begged, they would not let her marry Pio now.

That night Magda saw Pio and told him the news. "They can bring as many young men as they like," she said. "I won't marry any one of them. But we have to be more careful now that they know. It will be a lot more difficult for us to meet."

"I've been thinking about that," Pio said, "and I know just the place for us to go. There's a cave behind the Pagsanjan Falls. It's quite easy to get in, once you know the way."

So Pio and Magda met in the cave behind the waterfall. Meantime Magda's parents totally opposed her marriage to Pio, and Pio's parents refused to even consider the idea. "She's not for you," Pio's father said, "and I forbid you to see her."

Magda's parents looked for young men for her to marry. There were many fine-looking youths, and Magda politely considered each one. They were all good young men, honest and strong, but they were not Pio. He was the only one she would marry. She spent her time either thinking about Pio or plotting ways to go to their cave to meet him.

At last Magda's parents said, "We're tired of your behavior. You have to choose a young man and settle down." Magda turned her face away and refused to speak.

Later, Magda's mother said to her father, "I'm sure that she's still meeting Pio. He just isn't good enough for her! She's such a wonderful young woman, I can't bear to think of her throwing herself away on him."

The next day her mother watched Magda closely. She saw her daughter dress herself carefully, put a flower in her hair, and go to the Pagsanjan Falls. The mother followed. She soon knew of the lovers' meeting place behind the waterfall.

The day after this discovery, Magda's father spoke to her. "My dear," he said, "I know you think you love this young man. Believe me, he is no good for you. No member of his family has ever done a good thing for one of us, and some of them have been our enemies. Indeed, the two families survive because they have nothing to do with each other, so you must not see Pio anymore. And to be sure of that, you are not to leave the village. I want to be able to see where you are all day, every day. Now go to your grandmother. She is waiting for you, and she will be with you all the time."

Magda went obediently to her grandmother and did just what the old woman told her. Beneath her serene face lay a deep determination. She would run away with Pio—maybe tonight, maybe tomorrow night, but they would run away together.

At last the opportunity came, and Magda slipped away from her sleeping grandmother. Staying in the shadows, she crept around the village and began to walk toward the falls. She did not know that her father was following her, moving silently through the forest.

Magda reached the base of the waterfall and began the long climb to the cave. She listened carefully, but she heard nothing, for her father was a skillful hunter. He made no sound as he followed her into the cave where Pio lay sleeping.

"Pio!" Magda cried as she ran forward to kiss him. As the two embraced, her father burst into the cave. Pio turned to face him, but the man seized him and pushed him to the mouth of the cave, high above the water. Then he looked at Magda and pushed Pio out so that for one second he was framed in the moonlight. Then Pio was not there, and Magda knew without looking that he had died in his terrible fall.

Magda walked slowly to the door of the cave. She turned and looked sadly at her father. Her face seemed to say that nothing surprised her, that she had known that her story would end like this. Then, before he could touch her, she jumped into the void below.

The gods, who are wiser than mortals, turned the lovers into rocks which lie forever at the base of the waterfall. The people call the falls Magdapio.

Magda and Pio are together at last. ▲

Understanding What You Read

Read the following three accounts of the story and choose the one that is the most accurate. Be prepared to explain your choice to the rest of the class.

1. There was once a family who had a beautiful daughter, Magda. She fell in love with a young man called Pio. Her parents were delighted, because Pio was all they could ask for in a son-in-law. However, there was a terrible accident, and Pio and Magda were killed.

2. There once was a family who had a very special daughter, Magda. They wanted her to marry the best and bravest man in the world; but she had fallen in love with Pio, an ordinary young man, who loved her deeply in return. At last Magda's father killed Pio, and Magda fell to her death beside her lover.

3. There once was a family who dearly loved their daughter, Magda, and wanted a very special husband for her. Many young men came to her village, but she wanted only to marry Pio, who loved her deeply. Her family decided that it was best for the two lovers to be allowed to marry, and they lived happily ever after.

Vocabulary

Crossword Puzzle

Make up the clues to go with this crossword puzzle:

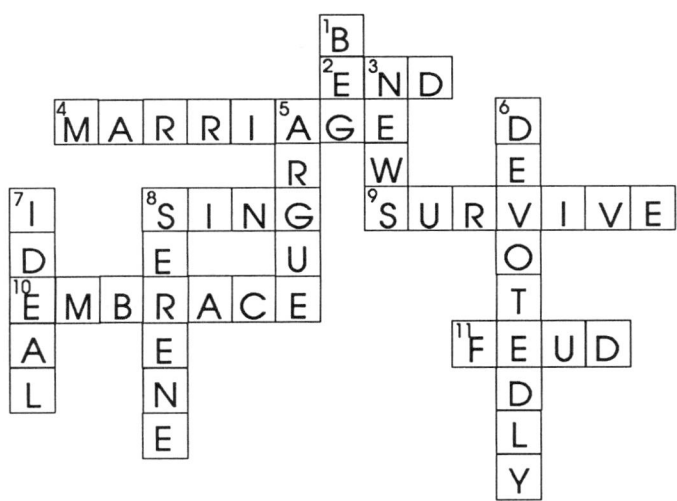

Across	Down
2.	1.
4.	3.
8.	5.
9.	6.
10.	7.
11.	8.

Tic-Tac-Toe

You should be in two teams. Team A has 30 seconds to choose a square and make up a sentence using the word in that square. Team B has 30 seconds to decide whether the sentence is correct and, if not, to correct it. The teacher will then put an A next to the word in the grid if the sentence was really correct. If it was wrong, and Team B corrected it properly, the teacher will put a B next to the word. The first team to get three letters in a row, diagonally, vertically, or horizontally, wins.

constantly	joy	disposition
exist	opposes	forbid
plot	arrange	honest

Discussion and Writing

Why do you think that Pio's family and Magda's family refused to have any contact with each other? Talk with your classmates, and then write a story that tries to explain the feud.

Scene from a Play

Pretend you are Magda and her grandmother. The grandmother has to keep Magda busy, and watch her all the time; but she's afraid she'll go to sleep and Magda will escape. Magda is very obedient, but she's waiting for her chance . . .

Work with a classmate and write a scene. Then act it out.

Tell It Your Way

Do you know any special love stories ? Tell them to your partner or to the class.

Change the story. Pio is awake when Magda's father enters the cave. The two men fight, and . . .

Write a story showing what happened. Work with a partner if you wish.

Outside the Story

Listening: Which Word Did You Hear Twice?

Many words in English have just one sound that makes them different from another word. Below you will find a list of words with just one sound difference. Your teacher will read the words to you, repeating one of the words twice. Circle the word that you hear twice. For example, if your teacher reads, "seal, seal, zeal," you will circle the word *seal*.

seal	zeal		sip	zip
sewn	zone		sounds	zounds
sing	zing		Sue	zoo
sink	zinc		see	zee

Library Work

Find the story of Romeo and Juliet, by William Shakespeare. How is it like the story of Magda and Pio?

Is there a special landmark in your district? Describe it and explain why you chose it. Try to make up a story about the landmark.

THE STORY OF BRAVE KONG

Before You Read

- Answer the following questions.

    1. Do you think Brave Kong is really brave? Explain your answer.
    2. What do you see in the illustration?

- Find Cambodia on the map at the front of the book. Then fill in the blanks below.

    1. Cambodia is to the south of _____ and _____.
    2. It is to the west of _____.
    3. It has access to the sea at the Gulf of _____.

Using What You Know

- Some animals make sounds that humans also make. Match each animal below (1–8) to its sound (a–h). If you need help, use your dictionary. (Remember to look up the *sound*, not the animals.)

_____	1. bears	a.	hiss
_____	2. parrots	b.	growl
_____	3. cats	c.	neigh
_____	4. pigs	d.	laugh
_____	5. horses	e.	squawk
_____	6. dogs	f.	grunt
_____	7. hyenas	g.	bark
_____	8. snakes	h.	mew

- Show your teacher what the following sounds mean.

    growl   howl   grunt   scream   gasp

    When do people make these sounds?

- Look up the words *brave* and *cowardly* in a thesaurus. How many of the words do you recognize?

There was once a Cambodian man called Brave Kong. He was a farmer, and he became a famous general in the Cambodian army. This is how it all happened.

Kong had two wives, Ahm and Kum. One day the three set out on a journey to another city. They had to pass through unknown country, so they were very alert and watchful. However, the trip was uneventful until they came to a village at the edge of a forest.

"I must warn you," one of the village women told Ahm. "There's a terrible tiger in the hills ahead of you. It has carried off goats and children, and it even attacks grown men. Be very careful, for this is no ordinary beast."

Ahm told Kum and Kong about the tiger, and they agreed to watch carefully. The next day they were in the forest when they heard a rumbling growl. An enormous tiger stood in their path.

Quickly Kong ran away and climbed into a hollow tree. He slid down inside and shook with terror. Horrible noises came from outside: growls and howls and the sound of someone beating a piece of wood on flesh. He imagined the tiger tearing poor Ahm and Kum apart. He hid deeper in his log as he heard grunts and screams. At last there was silence, broken only by heavy breathing and gasping. He thought the tiger was having trouble breathing after eating his wives. Then everything was quiet, and Kong decided the animal was probably too full to chase him. He peeped out of his hollow tree.

Ahm and Kum were sitting beside the dead tiger. Each woman held a piece of wood with blood on it. They were still breathing hard after the terrible fight.

Kong jumped out of his hollow tree and broke a stick off a tree. He began to beat the tiger. "I'll kill it," he cried. "What a huge brute!"

Ahm and Kum looked at him wearily. "Why did you run away and leave us?" Kum asked.

"I was getting my stick to kill the animal," Kong said.

"Why did you hide?" Kum asked.

"I wasn't hiding," Kong said. "See, I killed the tiger. I finished the beast off. What more can you ask?"

Ahm and Kum looked at each other. "I can ask for a brave husband," said Kum.

"You left us to die," Ahm said. "You are a coward, a weak, lily-livered coward!"

Just then another traveler came past. He saw the dead tiger, so he ran to Kong and said, "Thank you! You have killed the tiger that has terrorized our village."

Kum started to explain, "We killed the tiger. . ." but before she could say anymore, the foolish stranger laughed. He said, "Women can't kill tigers. Maybe you helped this man when the tiger was nearly dead." Then he turned to Kong and said, "Wait until we get to my home. People will dance for joy."

So Kong tore some vines from a tree and lashed the tiger to a pole. Ahm and Kum carried it into town. Everyone was very excited, and they made a hero of Kong and called him "Brave Kong, the tiger killer." Ahm and Kum were very tired, and they went to sleep quite early. The rest of the people, however, danced and feasted into the night. Soon Kong believed he *had* killed the tiger. "There I was," he told the people, "alone in the forest, for my wives had fled. I took a piece of wood, and I hit the tiger on the head, behind the ears. It tried to slash me with its claws, but I jumped away. Then I hit it again, and again . . ." Every time he told the story he became braver and more heroic.

This was big news, of course, and soon the king heard about brave Kong. When a fierce army gathered to attack Cambodia, the king said to his advisers, "Go and find Brave Kong. He can save us."

So Kong and his two wives came to the court. The king gave Kong a war elephant trained for battle and put him in command of the army. His two wives rode behind him.

Kong sat on his elephant at the front of his troops and was so scared that he felt sick. The enemy troops were approaching across the valley, and there were thousands of them. Kong wanted to turn around and run away, but Ahm and Kum wouldn't let him. Kong was so frightened that he shook. His arms jerked up and down by his sides, and his legs bumped against the head of his elephant.

The elephant felt the banging legs and thought it was a signal to run forward. It rushed toward the enemy, and Kong screamed in fear. Kong's soldiers heard his high-pitched screams. They thought it was a war cry. They saw Kong's elephant rushing into battle, so they followed.

Kong was getting closer to the enemy. Now he knew he was going to be sick from terror, and he leaned forward and vomited on the elephant's head. The animal ran faster, Kong's soldiers followed as closely as they could, and the enemy turned and ran away. It was a great victory.

Later, a soldier asked, "Brave Kong, does your battle cry always sound like a cry for help?"

Kong smiled a secret smile. "I ask the gods to bless me," he said modestly.

"Brave Kong, you were sick on your elephant's head," another soldier said. "Why was that so?"

"I was sick with excitement," Kong replied. "I did not get off my elephant because I wanted to go straight into battle." Kong looked around for Ahm and Kum. They weren't there, so he boasted and bragged about his courage.

The soldiers decided that Kong was very noble and dedicated. When they heard about a vicious crocodile, they came straight to Kong.

"There is a huge crocodile in the river," they said. "It takes men, women, and children. The people of the place can do nothing, so we told them about you. They're coming to ask for your help."

Kong was very worried. When the villagers came, they told him terrible stories about the crocodile. Kong felt worse than before. He consulted Ahm and Kum, and they decided that Kong must go to the river.

"You are the only one who can save us," the head man of the village said. So poor Kong went to the river where the huge crocodile was sleeping. It was resting just under a branch that was shaped like a V.

Kong stood with Ahm and Kum beside him, looking into the water. He knew he was going to die. He felt faint, and he staggered and fell deep into the river with a loud splash.

The crocodile awoke and jumped up. Its head got caught in the branch, and it could go neither forward nor backward.

Kong came up from the bottom of the river because he needed air. He saw that the crocodile was stuck. Quickly, Ahm and Kum gave him a lance and called out, "Kill it! Now!" Kong stabbed the crocodile's throat before it could bite him. The people cheered.

"Did you see the way Brave Kong jumped into the water?" they asked each other. "He pushed the crocodile up from beneath so it got caught on that branch. He's not just brave, he's very clever."

So Brave Kong had more stories to tell, and every time he told them they got bigger and sillier. But his wives, Ahm and Kum, didn't talk very much at all. They just smiled very quietly and listened to the stories that Brave Kong told. And, of course, people soon understood what really happened. Now everyone laughs when they hear the story of poor Brave Kong, who wasn't brave at all! ▲

Understanding What You Read

Tell the story to your partner. Which part did your partner think was funny? Which parts did other people in the class find funny? Ask three students, and write down what you found funny on the chart.

Name of student	Part they found funny
• Your partner	
• Student 1	
• Student 2	
• Student 3	
• You	

OR

Illustrate the part of the story you found most amusing. Write a few lines about it under the picture. Look at the pictures the other people in your group drew. Decide whose picture comes first in the story, whose comes second, and so on.

Vocabulary

• Two of the three words on each line have something in common. Identify the word that is different and explain why.

1.	enormous	huge	quiet
2.	animal	tiger	beast
3.	grunts	silence	screams
4.	weak	brave	heroic
5.	sick	scared	frightened
6.	vicious	noble	cruel
7.	bless	boast	brag
8.	sleeping	resting	gasping
9.	caught	stuck	dead
10.	talk	tell	smile

• Look back through the story to find words and phrases that describe how people feel and behave when they are fighting. Then write a description of Ahm and Kum fighting the tiger.

• Now write a description of how Kong felt when he was riding the elephant into battle.

Tall Stories

Make up some ridiculous questions and answers with your partner. For example:

Question: Have you ever shaken hands with a shark?

Answer: No, but I've danced with a whale!

Here are some verbs you can use, or you may think of your own.

met   eaten   flown   beaten   kissed

Discussion and Writing

- This story is a joke, because someone as lazy and frightened as Kong could not really succeed. Go through the story and find times when Ahm and Kum do things that make Kong look brave and clever.

- What advice would you give to people who wanted Brave Kong to help them?

- Brave Kong is an ironic story. It is amusing because it is obvious that Kong is a coward. Do you know any other ironic, back to front, unbelievable stories like this one? If so, tell the story to your partner or to the class.

Tell It Your Way

Pretend you are Ahm and Kum. Tell your story to the class.

OR

Pretend you are a journalist who has found the truth about Kong. Write a newspaper article about his life.

Outside the Story

Go to the library and ask for the story of "The Little Tailor," or "Seven at One Blow." How is it similar to Brave Kong? How is it different?

Limericks

There was a young lady from Niger
Who went for a ride on a tiger
They returned from the ride
With the lady inside
And a smile on the face of the tiger.

—Edward Lear

There was a young man from New York
Who always delighted in talk.
He chattered and chattered
The silence he shattered
'Til someone said "Shut up! You dork!"

Can you see how the rhyme works in a limerick? The last words of the first, second, and fifth line usually rhyme. In this limerick they are *York, talk,* and *dork.* The third and fourth lines are usually shorter than the others, and the last words rhyme. Here they are *chattered* and *shattered.*

Work with your classmates and make up some limericks.

Listening: Which Word Did You Hear Twice?

Many words in English have just one sound that makes them different from another word. Below you will find a list of words with just one sound difference. Your teacher will read the words to you, repeating one of the words twice. Circle the word that you hear twice. For example, if your teacher reads, "cat, cat, cot," you will circle the word *cat.*

cat	cot		axe	ox
cap	cop		map	mop
tap	top		lag	log
hat	hot		rat	rot
sad	sod		bag	bog

THE STORY OF RAMA AND SITA: RAVANA CAPTURES SITA

Before You Read

- Answer the following question.

  1. What do you see in the illustration?

- Find India on the map at the front of the book, and write a description of the country. Mention its size, and name the countries that are its neighbors.

Using What You Know

The story of Rama and Sita comes from the Ramayana, a very old epic poem about the conflict between good and evil. (An epic is a long poem about the deeds of gods and great people.) Think of all the words that you know that relate to goodness. Write them in the column on the left. Write words that relate to evil in the column on the right.

goodness	evil

eople started telling the story of Rama more than 3,000 years ago. As time went on, the poem called the Ramayana grew longer and more beautiful. This is a small part of the story.

King Dasaratha sent his son Prince Rama away from the palace and his homeland into exile. Rama could not return for fourteen years. Although King Dasaratha condemned only Rama, Rama's wife, Sita, and his brother, Lakshmana, would not hear of Rama staying alone.

"I am your wife," Sita said, "and I shall never leave your side. I made that promise at our wedding. How can you ask me to stay at the palace? I do not want to be without you for fourteen long years."

Lakshmana said, "I will come with you to help and protect you. It is unfair and unjust to send you away. I will share your exile with you." And the three set out. While the people of the country wept because their good Prince Rama was being so cruelly used, they rejoiced that Lakshmana and Sita were with the prince.

The forest was peaceful and beautiful, and the three lived happily, although they missed the many comforts of the palace. Rama, Sita, and Lakshmana moved deeper and deeper into the woods. Lakshmana built a house wherever they stayed. They lived simply, sleeping on grass mats on the ground and gathering food from the forest.

They were not alone, for holy men lived in the forest to meditate and to think about good and evil. One day Rama, Sita, and Lakshmana came upon such a holy man. He greeted them most kindly. They stayed with him for many months and learned from his wisdom and goodness.

At last the holy man told them it was time to go to a beautiful place, deep in the forest. He described the fruit and flowers they would see and gave them all his blessing. The holy man gave Rama special advice. "The future will be difficult, my son," the holy man said. "Some day you must fight Ravana, the King of Evil. Ravana has terrible powers, and you will need all the strength of goodness."

Rama, Sita, and Lakshmana walked on and on. They found the perfect place the holy man had talked about. Fruit trees grew by a clear stream, and birds sang sweetly to greet the morning sun as it touched the flowers. Peacocks perched in the trees, and wild deer grazed on the grass in the clearings. Lakshmana built a beautiful house near the stream, and the exiles spent the long summer at peace with all living creatures.

Autumn came, and the air grew cooler. Lakshmana found ice on the river when he went to fetch water in the mornings. The green lily leaves withered and turned brown with the cold. Evil began to stir. The demons became more active and tormented the holy men without pity. The King of the Demons, Ravana, moved about the world restlessly, terrifying all who saw him. Ravana was a monster with ten heads and twenty arms, and he knew that one day he must fight Rama.

Ravana had a sister, Surpa-nakha, a fearsome, ugly she-demon who changed her shape according to her mood. One day Surpa-nakha saw Rama in the forest and fell in love with him. "I have never seen such a man," she cried to herself. Love made her beautiful, and when she spoke to Rama, she was in the guise of a young girl. "I am Surpa-nakha, sister of Ravana," she proclaimed. "I choose you, Rama, to have the honor of being my husband." But nothing would take Rama away from Sita, and Surpa-nakha left angrily to plot a way to kill Sita and have Rama for herself.

Surpa-nakha soon thought of a plan. She came back to watch Rama's house, to catch a glimpse of his face, and to find out when Sita was alone and unguarded. At last she saw Sita leave the house to walk in the forest.

Sita found it difficult to remember that there could be danger in the midst of so much beauty, that a poisonous snake could lie in the grass, that evil as well as good moved in her world. Surpa-nakha followed Sita, ready to seize her, but Sita was unaware. As Surpa-nakha crept closer and closer to her victim, Sita had no idea of the danger she was in. Closer the she-demon came, like a tiger stalking a deer, closer and closer.

Lakshmana saw what was happening and ran to save Sita. Just as Surpa-nakha leapt on her prey, Lakshmana knocked her aside and Sita escaped.

The she-demon was very powerful, and she fought with all the strength of desperation. At last Lakshmana sliced off Surpa-nakha's nose and ears. The sky darkened to the color of blood, and Surpa-nakha ran to her brother's palace. "See what they have done to me?" she cried in rage to Ravana. "It's all because of the beautiful Sita."

Ravana listened carefully to his sister. He decided to see Sita for himself; he could add such a beauty to his wives. He told his sister he would send his army to punish Rama, Sita, and Lakshmana. He promised himself that he would rid the world of Rama so that he could keep Sita for his own.

Ravana's terrible army marched on Rama and Lakshmana and surrounded them. The battle lasted for seven days. When it was over, fourteen demon warlords and fourteen thousand demon warriors lay dead, yet Ravana was no closer than before to winning Sita. Even after the battle, he could not stop thinking about her. He knew he could not steal her away by force, so he decided to use trickery. He knew that Sita loved beautiful things.

One day a little golden deer appeared at the house where Rama, Sita, and Lakshmana lived. The creature was very pretty; its coat shone in the sun, and light sparkled from the sapphires on its horns. When Sita approached, it seemed quite unafraid, but it would not let her catch it.

"I wish I could have the little deer for a pet," Sita said wistfully. "See how its coat glows. It looks like silver and gold."

"I'll catch it for you," Rama replied, and he ran after the little deer.

The deer skipped into the forest. Whenever Rama got near, it slipped away into a darker place. Rama realized that it was leading him into a trap, and drew his bow to shoot the deer. As the deer fell, it called out in Rama's voice, "Help! Lakshmana! I'm hurt!"

Lakshmana heard the cry, and so did Sita. He did not want to leave Sita, but she begged him to go. "That was Rama's voice," she cried. "He's hurt! Please go to him! He needs you far more than I."

Lakshmana, deeply worried, ran to find his brother in the forest.

Meantime Ravana, the King of Demons, disguised himself so that he looked like an old beggar. He knocked on the door.

Sita greeted him kindly. "We do not see many people so deep in the forest," she said. "Are you tired? Have you traveled far?"

"I am tired, my child," said Ravana. "May I have some water?"

When Sita returned, Ravana seized her and forced her into his flying chariot. She cried out loudly, but there was nobody to hear. Ravana changed into his own form, and Sita saw his twenty arms and ten heads.

"Rama will save me!" she cried.

Ravana laughed and said, "Rama is dead." The chariot rose in the air.

An eagle, seeing Ravana steal Sita away, flew to help her. Ravana drew a sharp sword and cut off both its wings. The brave eagle fell to the ground.

Ravana turned the chariot toward the demon kingdom of Lanka. Although Sita was terrified, she was determined to leave a trail for Rama to follow. As they flew over a group of monkeys, she dropped her bracelets and her scarf. Then, half-fainting, she fell back against the cushions of the chariot. She could not see where the bangles fell, or whether the monkeys found them, but she clung to her hope: Rama would follow her, Rama would know where she had been taken.

Sita held onto one thought: Rama could not be dead. She refused to believe it, for if Rama were dead, there could be no joy left in Sita's life. ▲

Understanding What You Read

1. How long did Rama have to stay in exile?

2. What did Ravana's sister want?

3. How did Ravana trick Rama and Lakshmana away from Sita?

Vocabulary

Think of words that describe Rama and Ravana. Use them to make their names. The first two have been done for you:

```
B  R  A  V  E            S  T  R  O  N  G
   A                            A
   M                            V
   A                            A
                                N
                                A
```

Compare your list with what other people have written. Do you agree with the words they used? Can you justify the words you chose?

Discussion and Writing

1. Lakshmana is a personification of loyalty. What does loyalty mean to you? Give examples of loyalty from your own experience, or from stories you have heard or read.

2. Why do you think Rama was exiled? If you already know the story, work with other people who also know it. People who do not know the story should work together to think of possible reasons why Rama was unjustly sent into exile.

3. The three exiles missed the many comforts of the palace. What would life in the palace be like? What would they be doing without? Work with others in your class and make a list.

Tell It Your Way

Do you know any other stories about people being captured? If so, tell the story to your partner or to the class.

What will happen in the next chapter, "The Rescue" ? Ask the other people in your group. Make notes on what they think below. If you already know the story, work with other people who also know it, and see how many different variations of the story you know. People who do not know the story should work together. There are no absolutely right answers to this question.

Outside the Story

Haiku

Haiku is a form of poetry written in Japan. There are three lines in the poem: the first one is short, the second long, and the third short. (Actually, Haiku are written with five syllables in the first line, seven in the second and five in the third, but we don't have to follow this rule absolutely.)

Look back at your list of words relating to good and evil. Write your haiku with a short first line, a longer second line, and a short third line. Here's an example:

Evil Ravana

Deceives the gentle Sita

Creating great havoc

Library Work

Find out about India today. How many people live there? What sort of work do they do? What is life like for people in India today?

Listening: Which Word Did You Hear Twice?

Many words in English have just one sound that makes them different from another word. On the next page you will find a list of words with just one sound difference. Your teacher will read the words to you, repeating one of the words twice. Circle the word that you hear twice. For example, if your teacher reads, "thank, thank, tank," you will circle the word *tank*.

thank	tank	thorn	torn
theme	team	three	tree
thick	tick	threw	true
thin	tin	thug	tug
thong	tong	thrust	trust

Dictation

_____

_____

_____

_____

_____

_____

_____

_____

The Story of Rama and Sita: The Rescue

Before You Read

- Answer the following questions.

  1. What does the title mean?
  2. What do you see in the illustration?

- Find Sri Lanka on the map at the front of the book.

  1. What is the name of the strait between Sri Lanka and India?
  2. What is the capital of Sri Lanka?

Using What You Know

Think of what you have learned about Rama, Sita, Ravana, and Lakshmana from the last story. How do you expect them to behave?

ama and Lakshmana hurried back to the hut to find Sita, but she was gone.

"I knew it was a trick!" Lakshmana said. "Why did I leave her?"

"Why was I such a fool?" Rama asked, and he sank down on the floor of the house.

"Come along!" Lakshmana said urgently. "We must look for Sita. You're doing no good sitting still. We'll search all India, if we must."

At last Rama dragged himself to his feet, and the two brothers began their long search. Very soon they found the brave eagle, and it told them how it had tried to save Sita. As the eagle finished speaking, the great bird died.

Rama and Lakshmana moved on, asking everyone they met if they had seen Sita. At last they met Hanuman, the monkey general, son of Vayu the Wind God. Hanuman was brave and good, cunning and clever, and noble in his behavior. His monkey army soon gave him news of a beautiful woman who dropped her scarf and necklace from a flying chariot. Then more news came: an eagle said that it saw the chariot flying across the sea toward the island of Lanka, the stronghold of the wicked Ravana.

"Let me search for Sita on Lanka," Hanuman said to Rama. "Only give me a token, so Sita will know that I come from you." So Rama gave Hanuman a ring from his finger. Hanuman, using his magic powers, changed himself to an enormous size and went to the southern part of India. He looked across the sea to the island of Lanka. Hanuman summoned all his tremendous strength and leapt like a great bird across the sea from India to Lanka. He changed himself immediately to the size of a small cat and went to find Sita.

Ravana had imprisoned Sita with the most horrible she-demons. Hanuman crept among them and whispered Rama's name to Sita. Sita, made miserable in her captivity, did not understand who was talking at first. Then Hanuman gave her Rama's ring, and Sita's joy was unbounded. She took a jewel from a corner of her sari, and gave it to Hanuman.

"What are you doing?" one of the she-demons asked. "Why did you give that monkey a jewel? Catch him, quickly." The demons swooped on Hanuman and took him to Ravana.

"I come as a messenger from Rama," Hanuman told Ravana. "Rama demands that you return his wife Sita and that you stop your evil ways. If you do not, he will come to Lanka to destroy you. He will bring a great army."

"Stop!" roared Ravana. "I will be happy to fight him! Look what he did to my sister! Look what Rama and Lakshmana did to my fourteen demon warlords! But first, monkey, I am going to make a fool of you. My demons will take you through the city, and we will watch you dance. Bring me a pile of rags!"

A demon brought some rags, and Ravana tied them to Hanuman's tail. "Now bring me some oil!" Ravana cried.

Ravana poured oil on the rags. "Bring me some fire!" he ordered his demons. Slowly, so that he could inflict the most pain and fear, Ravana set fire to Hanuman's tail. The cruel demons laughed and dragged Hanuman into the street so that people could watch his ordeal.

Brave Hanuman watched the rags on his tail burn and smelled the fire, but it did not hurt him. Then he began to shrink until he was too small for his bonds to hold him. Slipping from the ropes and chains, he climbed onto the roofs of the city and returned to his usual size. He danced about merrily, setting fire to everything his tail touched from one end of the city to the other, causing panic and pandemonium. Then he sucked his tail to extinguish the flames, climbed a hill, and leapt back to India.

Rama was delighted to hear about Sita, and he and Lakshmana prepared for war. The Ape King Sugriva put all his troops at their disposal, and what troops they were! Bears with claws like razors, monkeys of every size and color, all sworn to help defeat Ravana, all led by the heroic Hanuman.

Ravana, safe on his island, laughed when his spies told him that the troops were gathering on the mainland. "How will they get here?" he asked. "They cannot swim so far, only Hanuman can jump from land to land, and they do not have enough boats. Let their forces assemble! They cannot cross the water."

But even as he spoke, the monkeys and bears were gathering rocks to build a bridge from India to Lanka. Thousands upon thousands of monkeys and bears threw rocks into the sea. The bridge came closer and closer to Lanka.

Ravana's army gathered, fearful of Rama, who had never been defeated in battle. Soon Rama's army crossed to Lanka on the monkeys' bridge. The battle began, and it was fierce and long.

The demons used magic invisible snake arrows to attack Rama and Lakshmana. These arrows turned into deadly snakes, and nobody could see where they came from, or how to combat them. The snakes bit Rama and Lakshmana until they were nearly dead.

Ravana put Sita into a flying chariot and made her look down. "See, your husband Rama is dying," Ravana said. Then he took her away.

As Sita wept with fear for Rama and his loyal brother Lakshmana, a huge eagle came to their rescue. The eagle terrified the snakes, and they slithered away from Rama and Lakshmana, who recovered immediately.

The battle raged on, and at last Rama and Ravana came to fight in single combat. Rama chased Ravana all around the world, and the thunder rolled as they fought. Rama cut off one of Ravana's heads, and another head grew back, with eyes that looked at the world even more hatefully than before. The sky grew dark and angry-looking, and Ravana called more poisonous snakes and dragons to fight against Rama. Rama turned these evil reptiles aside with holy power, and the battle raged on and on until Rama used the power of good to help him kill Ravana by destroying his evil heart with a flaming arrow tip. The battle was over.

So peace came to Lanka, and Rama and Sita were reunited. The fourteen years exile were over, and Rama, Sita, and the faithful Lakshmana returned to their own land. They were met by the rejoicing of the people. ▲

Understanding What You Read

1. Tell the story to your partner. Which part did your partner think was the most exciting? Which part did your partner think was the most moving? Make notes below, and find out what other people in the class thought.

2. Match the beginnings and ends of these sentences.

_____ 1. Ravana captured Sita   a. to Hanuman's tail.

_____ 2. Hanuman the monkey general   b. a terrible battle.

_____ 3. Hanuman found Sita   c. to fight with Rama.

_____ 4. The she-demons caught Hanuman   d. by using a trick.

_____ 5. Ravana said he would be glad   e. and gave her Rama's ring.

_____ 6. Ravana set fire   f. leapt from India to Lanka.

_____ 7. Rama and Ravana fought   g. and took him to Ravana.

Vocabulary

1. Think of words that describe Sita and Lakshmana. Use them to make their names. Two of them have been done for you:

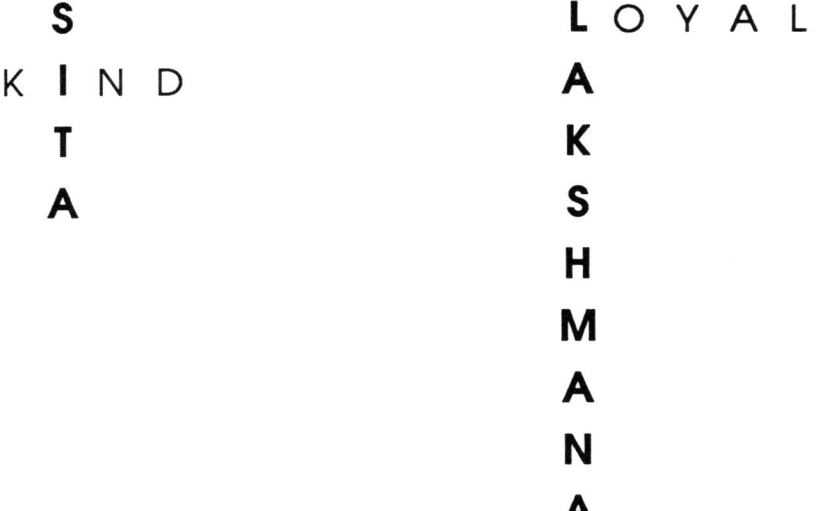

```
        S                      L O Y A L
    K  I  N  D                 A
        T                      K
        A                      S
                               H
                               M
                               A
                               N
                               A
```

Compare your list with what other people have written. Do you agree with the words they've used? Can you justify the words you chose?

2. Read the sentences. Circle the letter for the correct meaning of the underlined words. Use the meaning from the story.

   1. Rama <u>sank down</u> on the floor of the house.
      a. lay down slowly
      b. fell down
      c. looked down

   2. At last Rama <u>dragged himself to his feet</u>.
      a. stood up quickly
      b. stood up slowly and with difficulty
      c. dragged himself across the floor

   3. "Give me <u>a token</u>, so Sita will know that I come from you."
      a. something small
      b. something valuable
      c. something she will know is yours

4. Hanuman gave Sita Rama's ring, and <u>her joy was unbounded</u>.
   a. She was extremely worried.
   b. She was extremely happy.
   c. She didn't know what to think.

5. But first, monkey, I am going <u>to make a fool of you</u>.
   a. to make people trick you
   b. to make people laugh at you
   c. to make people follow you

6. The thunder <u>rolled</u> as they fought.
   a. made a loud noise
   b. moved around
   c. stopped

Discussion and Writing

Why do you think people have enjoyed this story for 3,000 years?

The Five Senses: How Ideas Can Fit Together

Work with a classmate and answer the following questions. Be prepared to explain your choices to the rest of the class. (There are no absolutely right or wrong answers.)

Here is an example of what one student wrote for truth.

What would truth sound like?	*a ringing bell*
What color would truth be?	*pure white*
What would truth taste like?	*wine*
What would truth smell like?	*fresh flowers*
What would truth feel like?	*new paper*

What would loyalty sound like?
What color would loyalty be?
What would loyalty taste like?
What would loyalty smell like?
What would loyalty feel like?

What would courage sound like?
What color would courage be?
What would courage taste like?
What would courage smell like?
What would courage feel like?

What would evil sound like?
What color would evil be?
What would evil taste like?
What would evil smell like?
What would evil feel like?

TELL IT YOUR WAY

1. Do you know any stories about a rescue? If so, tell the story to your partner or class.

2. Mime the following parts of the story.
    a. When Hanuman found Sita
    b. When Ravana showed Sita, Rama, and Lakshmana lying on the ground close to death

3. Make a wanted poster for Ravana. Describe him. List his crimes.

    OR

    Prepare a tribute to Hanuman, listing his achievements and his personal qualities.

4. Role-play the part of the story when Hanuman gave Rama's message to Ravana, and Ravana set fire to Hanuman's tail.

Outside the Story

Library Work

Find out what happened to Sita after her reunion with Rama.

OR

What do geographers believe to be the cause of the islands between India and Sri Lanka?

Listening: Which Word Did You Hear Twice?

Many words in English have just one sound that makes them different from another word. Below you will find a list of words with just one sound difference. Your teacher will read the words to you, repeating one of the words twice. Circle the word that you hear twice. For example, if your teacher reads, "wail, veil, veil," you will circle the word *veil*.

wail	veil
Walt	vault
wane	vane
wend	vend
went	vent
wet	vet
wine	vine
worse	verse
wow	vow
west	vest

Game

Write a sentence on a piece of paper that begins a story about a rescue. Pass it to the person next to you. That person reads your sentence, adds another sentence, and passes it on to the next person. The last person hands the piece of paper back to you, and you read the story.

Suggested Reading for the Teacher

 ou may like to read these references to learn more about folk stories from Asia and ways to use those stories in the classroom.

Chi Do, Supervisor. *A Collection of Papers in Vietnamese Culture, Book II.* Indochinese Culture Center, Houston, 1981.

Clarkson, Atelia and Cross, Gilbert. *World Folktales: A Scribner Resource Collection.* Charles Scribner's Sons, New York, 1980.

Dorson, Richard M. *Folk Legends of Japan.* Charles E. Tuttle, 1962.

Duong Duc Nhu, Supervisor. *A Collection of Papers in Vietnamese Culture.* Indochinese Culture Center, Houston, 1981.

Eberhard, Wolfram, Editor. *Folktales of China.* University of Chicago Press, 1965.

Frank, Rinvolucri, Berer. *Challenge to Think.* O.U.P. 1982.

Gan, Linda. *A Treasury of Asian Folktales*, Dominie Press, 1992.

Gavin, Jamila. *Three Indian Princesses.* Methuen, 1987.

Greenwood, Jean. *Class Readers.* O.U.P., 1988.

Lindstrom, Seth, Editor. The *Recipe Book.* Longman, 1990.

Mitford, A.B. *Tales of Old Japan.* Charles E. Tuttle, 1966.

Monteiro, Irene-Anne. *Favourite Stories from Old Korea.* Heinemann Educational Books (Asia) Ltd, 1984.

Ozaki, Yei Theodora. *The Japanese Fairy Book.* Charles E. Tuttle, 1970.

Rinvolucri, Mario. *Grammar Games.* C.U.P., 1984.

Sechrist, Betty Lou and Moua, Dang. *Lao-English Legends.* Long Beach Unified School District, California.

Siek, Marguerite. *Favourite Stories from Indonesia.* Heinemann Educational Books (Asia) Ltd 1972.

Thompson, Brian. *The Story of Prince Rama.* Viking Kestrel, 1980.

Ram, Govinder. *Rama and Sita.* Blackie and Son, 1987.

Bridge Across Asia
Answer Key

How Vietnamese People Discovered Watermelons

p. 1: Before You Read
1. A watermelon is a large, juicy, sweet fruit, usually with red flesh or pulp. The pulp is usually riddled with black seeds.
2. Answers will vary.

The paragraph should read as follows:
Vietnam is a <u>country</u> in Asia. Its nearest neighbors are China, which is on its <u>northern</u> border, and Laos and <u>Kampuchea</u>, which are west of Vietnam. The Gulf of <u>Tonkin</u>, which is part of the <u>Pacific</u> Ocean, is to the east of Vietnam. The country is close to the equator, so it is very hot. The language of Vietnam is called <u>Vietnamese</u>, although some Vietnamese people speak Cantonese, which is the language of southern China.

p. 2: -*B.C.* means "before Christ." *A.D.* means "*anno Domini*, in the year of our Lord."
-4,834
-Approximately 2,263 years ago, depending on the year in which you are reading this book.

Using What You Know
1. The *mainland* means
   b. a large landmass without its islands
2. Do things for myself; alone, independent, loneliness, hot, scared, frightened, self-sufficient, etc.
3. Shelter, clean water, fishing tackle, food

p. 5: Understanding What You Read
Part I:
1. adopted
2. everything
3. furious
4. island
5. watermelons
6. mainland
7. mainland

Part II: Answers will vary.
Vocabulary
1. e
2. g
3. f
4. b
5. c
6. a
7. d

pp. 6–7: Answers will vary.

Why the Moon Goes Away

p. 8: Before You Read
1. Answers will vary.
2. Answers will vary.
3. A chariot is used for transportation.

Thailand is surrounded by <u>Myanmar</u> to the north and west, by Laos to the northeast and by <u>Kampuchea</u> to the south and east. The northern part of Thailand is a peninsula that goes down to the border with <u>Malaysia</u>. The country is close to the equator, so it is very <u>hot</u>. The Andaman Sea lies <u>west</u> of Thailand.

p. 9: Using What You Know

moon	sun
bright	hot
changeable	gasses
craters	star
half	burning
quarter	day
whole	sky
new	
sky	
stars	

p. 12: Understanding What You Read
1. long ago, before the sun and the moon
2. The Sun King wouldn't go home with his chariot because he was in love with Tatsani.
3. Tatsani and the Sun King should marry but the Sun King must agree to go home at the end of every day and Tatsani must agree to become the moon to the stars.

Vocabulary
Answers will vary. The following are possible answers:
BEAU<u>T</u>IFUL
D<u>A</u>UGHTER
SWEE<u>T</u>
GRACIOU<u>S</u>
C<u>A</u>RING
GEN<u>T</u>LE
K<u>I</u>ND

pp. 13–16: Answers will vary.

The Story of the Mount of Anticipation, Mother-Son Mountain
Before You Read

p. 17: 1–3. Answers will vary.
   • China, Thailand, the Philippines, Malaysia; over the ocean, by boat

p. 18: Using What You Know

words about feelings	words about the sea
grief	sail
restless	sailor
cheerful	boat
joy	ship
glad	

p. 21: Answers will vary. The following are possible answers:

Vocabulary

Across:
4. Came out of a deep sleep
5. Harshly, strongly
6. To feel sorry for
7. To walk in a sneaky way
8. Sounds of footfalls

Down:
1. Without company of any kind
2. Middle
3. Unable to settle in one place

pp. 22–24: Answers will vary.

The Golden Swan

p. 25: Before You Read
1. Answers will vary.
2. Answers will vary.

p. 26:
1. Vietnam
2. Myanmar
3. North
4. No
5. Hot, humid, equatorial

p. 29: Vocabulary
1. took to his bed
2. nursed him devotedly
3. slipped back
4. did not know how to live without him
5. tossed and turned in her sleep
6. wept with gratitude
7. possessed by greed

pp. 29–31: Answers will vary.

The Elves Help an Old Man

p. 32: Before You Read
1. Short, small
2. Answers will vary.

1. North and South Korea
2. Sea of Japan
3. Pacific Ocean
4. No. It is not as close to the equator.
5. The sun rises in the east.

p. 33: Using What You Know
The following words are likely to be underlined: jump, lightly, music, waltz, fiddle, hop, jive, square dance, steps, jig, disco, bow to somebody, rest, rhythm. Answers may include stretch, sweat, posture, costumes, practice, perform, performance, shoes, tap, ballet, modern, jazz, ballroom, tango, etc.

p. 37: Understanding What You Read
1. ugly
2. hide
3. elves
4. come back
5. hurried
6. neighbors
7. forest
8. swelling

Vocabulary
1. a
2. c
3. a
4. c
5. b
6. b
7. c

• The man was fun, friendly, generous and could make other people happy; he also had a growth on his face that upset him quite a bit.

pp. 38–39: Answers will vary.

The Story of White Onion and Red Onion

p. 40: Before You Read
1. a child of a husband or wife by a subsequent marriage; a wife of one's father by a subsequent marriage; a daughter of one's parent by a subsequent marriage
2. Answers will vary.

p. 41: Answers will vary. The following are possible answers:
1. coconuts, fruit, ride
2. Yes, because they are surrounded by water.
3. Saris, shorts, skirts, cotton pants, short-sleeved shirts

p. 45: Understanding What You Read
The order should be as follows:
2, 3, 7, 4, 6, 1, 5

Vocabulary
1. protect her
2. work for your living

p. 46:
3. wondered
4. hurry up
5. a life of ease
6. the keeper
7. drowned
8. grew impatient
9. peered

pp. 46–48: Answers will vary.

The Animals of the Chinese Zodiac

p. 49: Before You Read
1–3. Answers will vary.
4. the animals of the Chinese zodiac

p. 54: Understanding What You Read
1. snakes
2. rabbits
3. horses
4. pigs
5. dogs
6. goats
7. oxen
8. roosters
9. dragons
10. monkeys
11. tigers
12. rats

p. 55: Vocabulary
Across:
4. kind
5. charming
8. creative
9. bold
10. expensive
11. tactful

Down:
1. steadily
2. advise
3. confident
6. intelligent
7. active

pp. 56–57: Answers will vary.

The Woodcutter in the Moon

p. 58: Before You Read
1. Answers will vary.
2. Answers will vary.

1. three times bigger
2. cold
3. hot
4. Answers will vary.

p. 59: Using What You Know
1. They are all about birds.
2. amazed, astonished, dazzled

p. 61: Understanding What You Read
A. nursed it tenderly
B. let it go
C. seed
D. a pumpkin
E. injured
F. an old man
G. He cut down a cinnamon tree.
H. A rooster pecked him and the wood of the tree grew back together again.

p. 62: Vocabulary
1. e
2. a
3. g
4. b
5. f
6. c
7. d

pp. 63–64: Answers will vary.

The Flying Fairy Wife

p. 66: Before You Read
1. Answers will vary.
2. Answers will vary.

1. China
2. East
3. Sea of Japan
4. Pacific
5. Isthmus

p. 67: Using What You Know
1. c
2. f
3. d
4. e
5. a
6. b

p. 70: Understanding What You Read
The order should be as follows:
5, 6, 3, 4, 1, 2

Vocabulary
1. a
2. a
3. c
4. b
5. a
6. c

pp. 71–72: Answers will vary.

The Legend of Magdapio

p. 73: Before You Read
1. Answers will vary.
2. China, Vietnam, Malaysia, Singapore; Answers will vary.

pp. 76–77: Understanding What You Read
#2 should be circled.

Vocabulary
Answers will vary. The following are possible answers:

Across:
2. the opposite of the beginning
4. another word for wedlock
8. to vocally talk to the tune of music
9. to live
10. to hug
11. a long-standing fight between family members or neighbors

Down:
1. to ask for money or food
3. the latest information of the day
5. fight
6. lovingly, with loyalty
7. a standard of perfection
8. calm and peaceful

pp. 78–79: Answers will vary.

The Story of Brave Kong

p. 80: Before You Read
1. Answers will vary.
2. Answers will vary.

1. Thailand; Laos.
2. Vietnam
3. Tonkin

p. 81: Using What You Know
1. b
2. e
3. h
4. f
5. c
6. g
7. d
8. a
Answers will vary.

p. 86: Vocabulary
Explanations of why the third word is different will vary. The following are possible answers:
1. quiet—The other two words are synonyms for "big."
2. tiger—Tiger is a specific name of a particular animal. The other two words are general descriptions of animals.
3. silence—The other two words describe noises.
4. weak—The other two words describe bravery.
5. sick—The other two words are synonyms.
6. noble—The other two words are synonyms for mean.
7. bless—The other two words are synonyms.
8. gasping—The other two words describe someone at rest.
9. dead—The other two words are synonyms.
10. smile—The other two words are synonyms for speak.

pp. 86–88: (Remainder) Answers will vary.

The Story of Rama and Sita: Ravana Captures Sita

p. 89: Before You Read
1. Answers will vary.
2. Nepal, Bangladesh, China, Burma

p. 90: Using What You Know
Answers will vary.

p. 94: Understanding What You Read
1. 14 years
2. Rama to love her
3. He had a beautiful deer run past Sita, knowing she would ask Rama to catch it for her. As Rama chased the deer, the deer led him farther and farther away from Sita. Knowing he was being led into a trap, Rama shot the deer and it fell, calling out to Lakshmana in Rama's voice. Lakshmana ran to help his brother.

Vocabulary
Answers will vary. The following are possible answers:

BRAVE	STRONG
ADORED	AVARACIOUS
MALE	VENAL
ATTENTIVE	CRAZY
	NAUGHTY
	MEAN

pp. 94–96: (Remaining) Answers will vary.

The Story of Rama and Sita: The Rescue

p. 97: Before You Read
1. Answers will vary.
2. Answers will vary.

1. Palk Straight
2. Columbo

p. 100: Understanding What You Read
1. d
2. f
3. e
4. g
5. c
6. a
7. b

p. 101: Vocabulary
Answers will vary. The following are possible answers:

BEAUTEOUS	LOYAL
KIND	BRAVE
STUNNING	KIND
ADORED	STRONG
	HUMAN
	MALE
	CAPABLE
	HANDSOME
	FAITHFUL

1. a
2. b
3. c
4. b
5. b
6. b

pp. 102–104: Answers will vary.

1-800-321-3106
www.pearsonlearning.com

Dominie Press
Pearson Learning Group

PEARSON
Learning Group

ISBN 0-7685-5511-6

90000

9 780768 555110